DOUBLE FUDGE

Books by Judy Blume

The One in the Middle Is the Green Kangaroo
Freckle Juice

The Pain and the Great One series
Soupy Saturdays
Cool Zone
Going, Going, Gone!
Friend or Fiend?

The Fudge books
Tales of a Fourth Grade Nothing
Otherwise Known as Sheila the Great
Superfudge
Fudge-a-Mania
Double Fudge

For 9+ readers
Blubber
Iggie's House
Starring Sally J. Freedman as Herself
Are You There, God? It's Me, Margaret
It's Not the End of the World
Then Again, Maybe I Won't
Deenie
Just as Long as We're Together
Here's to You, Rachel Robinson

For teens
Tiger Eyes
Forever
Letters to Judy: What Kids Wish They Could Tell You

Judy Blume

A FUDGE BOOK

DOUBLE FUDGE

MACMILLAN CHILDREN'S BOOKS

First published 2002 by Macmillan Children's Books

This edition published 2014 by Macmillan Children's Books
an imprint of Pan Macmillan
20 New Wharf Road, London N1 9RR
Associated companies throughout the world
www.panmacmillan.com

ISBN 978-1-4472-6288-6

3 5 7 9 8 6 4

A CIP catalogue record for this book is available from
the British Library.

Printed and bound by CPI Group (UK) Ltd, Croydon CR0 4YY

For my grandson Elliot,
who lights up my life

Contents

1
The Miser

When my brother Fudge was five, he discovered money in a big way. 'Hey, Pete,' he said one night as I was getting out of the shower. 'How much would it cost to buy New York?'

'The city or the state?' I asked, as if it were a serious question.

'Which is bigger?'

'The state, but all the good stuff is in the city.' People who don't live in the city might disagree, but I'm a city kind of guy.

'We live in the city, right?' Fudge said. He was sitting on the open toilet seat in his pyjamas.

'You're not *doing* anything, are you?' I asked as I towelled myself dry.

'What do you mean, Pete?'

'I *mean* you're sitting on the toilet, and you haven't pulled down your PJs.'

He swung his feet and started laughing. 'Don't worry, Pete. Only Tootsie still poops in her pants.' Tootsie is our little sister. She'll be two in February.

Fudge watched as I combed my wet hair. 'Are you going someplace?' he asked.

'Yeah, to bed.' I got into clean boxers and pulled a T-shirt over my head.

'Then how come you're getting dressed?'

'I'm not getting dressed. Starting tonight, this is what I wear instead of pyjamas. And how come you're still up?'

'I can't go to sleep until you tell me, Pete.'

'Tell you what?'

'How much it would cost to buy New York City.'

'Well, the Dutch paid about twenty-four dollars for it back in the sixteen hundreds.'

'Twenty-four dollars?' His eyes opened wide. 'That's all?'

'Yeah, it was a real bargain. But don't get your hopes up. That's not what it would cost today, even if it were for sale, which it's not.'

'How do you know, Pete?'

'Believe me, I know!'

'But how?'

'Listen, Fudge, by the time you're twelve there's a lot of stuff you know, and you don't even know how you know it.'

He repeated my line. 'There's a lot of stuff you know, and you don't even know how you know it!' Then he laughed like crazy. 'That's a tongue-twister, Pete.'

'No, that's just the truth, Fudge.'

The next day he was at it again. In the elevator he asked Sheila Tubman, 'How much money do you have, Sheila?'

'That's not a polite question, Fudgie,' she told him. 'Nice people don't talk about their money, especially in these times.' Sheila gave me a look like it was my fault my brother has no manners. I hope she's not in my class this year. I hope that *every* year, and every year she's there, like some kind of itch you can't get rid of, no matter how hard you scratch.

'I'm nice,' Fudge said, 'and I like to talk about money. You want to know how much I have?'

'No,' Sheila told him. 'It's nobody's business but yours.'

He told her anyway. I knew he would. 'I have fourteen dollars and seventy-four cents. I mise my money every night before I go to sleep.'

'You *mise* your money?' Sheila asked. Then she shook her head at me like it's my fault he thinks mise is a word.

Henry, who runs the elevator in our building,

laughed. 'Nothing like having a miser in the family.'

'You don't have to be a miser, Fudge,' Sheila said. 'If you like counting money so much, you can work at a bank when you grow up.'

'Yeah,' Fudge said. 'I can work at a bank and mise my money all day long.'

Sheila sighed. 'He doesn't get it,' she said to me.

'He's only five,' I reminded her.

'Almost six,' he reminded me. Then he tugged Sheila's arm. 'Hey, Sheila, you know how much the Dude paid for New York City?'

'The Dude?' Sheila asked. 'Is this some kind of joke?'

'Not the *Dude*,' I told Fudge. 'The *Dutch*.'

'His name was Peter Minuit,' Sheila said, like the know-it-all she is. 'And he paid the Wappinger Indian tribe in trinkets, not cash. Besides, the Indians thought they were going

to share the land, not sell it.'

'Sharing is good,' Fudge said. 'Except for money. I'll never share my money. My money is all mine. I love my money!'

'That's a disgusting thing to say,' Sheila told him. 'You're not going to have any friends if you talk that way.'

By then the elevator reached the lobby. 'Your brother has no values,' Sheila said as we walked to the door of our building. Outside, she turned and headed towards Broadway.

'How much do *values* cost?' Fudge asked me.

'Not everything's for sale,' I told him.

'It should be.' Then he skipped down to the corner singing, '*Money, money, money, I love money, money, money . . .*'

That's when I knew we were in big trouble.

'It's just a stage,' Mom told me later when I pointed out that Fudge is obsessed by money.

'Maybe, but it's still embarrassing,' I said. 'You better do something before school starts.'

But Mom didn't take me seriously until that night at dinner when Dad said, 'Please pass the salt, Fudge.'

'How much will you give me for it?' Fudge asked. The saltshaker was sitting right in front of him.

'Excuse me,' Dad said. 'I'm asking for a favour, not hiring someone to do a job.'

'If you hire me I'll pass the salt,' Fudge said. 'How about a dollar?'

'How about nothing?' I said, reaching for the salt and passing it to Dad.

'No fair, Pete!' Fudge shouted. 'He asked me, not you.'

'Thank you, Peter,' Dad said and he and Mom shared a look.

'I told you, didn't I?' I said to them. 'I told you we have a big problem.'

7

'What problem?' Fudge asked.

'You!' I said.

'Foo!' Tootsie said from her high chair, as she threw a handful of rice across the table.

'What's the difference between dollars and bucks?' Fudge asked the next morning at breakfast. He was drawing dollar signs all over the Cheerios box with a red marker.

'Bucks is just another word for dollars,' Mom told him, moving the cereal box out of his reach.

'Nobody says bucks any more,' I said. 'Where'd you hear about bucks?'

'Grandma was reading me a story and the guy called his money bucks,' Fudge said. 'He had five bucks and he thought that was a lot. Is that funny or what?' He shovelled a handful of dry Cheerios into his mouth, then washed them down with a swig of milk. He refuses to mix his cereal and milk in a bowl like everyone else.

'Five dollars is nothing to sneeze at,' Dad said, carrying Tootsie into the kitchen. 'I remember saving for a model aeroplane that cost four dollars and ninety-nine cents, and in those days that *was* a lot.' Dad sat Tootsie in her high chair and doled out some Cheerios for her. 'Somebody's been decorating the cereal box,' he said.

'Yeah, the miser's learned to draw dollar signs,' I said.

It wasn't long before the miser started making his own money. 'Fudge Bucks,' he told us. 'I'm going to make a hundred million trillion of them.' And just like that, with one box of markers and a pack of coloured paper, he was on his way. 'Soon I'll have enough Fudge Bucks to buy the whole world.'

'Why don't you start with something smaller?' I suggested. 'You don't want to buy

the whole world right off because then you won't have anything to look forward to.'

'Good idea, Pete. I'll start with Toys 'R' Us.'

'The kid has no values,' I told my parents after Fudge went to bed. They looked at me like I was some kind of crazy. 'Well, he doesn't,' I said. 'He worships money.'

'I wouldn't go that far,' Dad said. 'It's not unusual for young children to want things.'

'I want things, too,' I reminded Dad. 'But I don't go around obsessing about money.'

'It's just a phase,' Mom said this time.

We could hear Fudge as he started to sing, '*Oh, money, money, money, I love money, money, money . . .*'

As soon as he stopped, Uncle Feather, his myna bird, started. 'Ooooo, money, money, money . . .'

Turtle, my dog, lifted his head and howled. He thinks he can sing.

10

Dad called, 'Fudge, cover Uncle Feather's cage and get to sleep.'

'Uncle Feather's *mising* his money,' Fudge called back. 'He's not ready to go to sleep.'

'How did this happen to us?' Mom asked. 'We've always worked hard. We spend carefully. And we never talk about money in front of the children.'

'Maybe that's the problem,' I told them.

2
Shoes and News

A couple of days before school started we went to Harry's, the shoe store on Broadway. When he was three, Fudge only wanted to wear the same shoes as me. Now he has his own ideas. But this time he couldn't decide between black with silver trim or white with blue; between lace-ups, velcro closings, or pull-ons; between hi-tops or low. 'I'll just get two pairs,' he told Mom. 'Maybe three.' He licked his yellow lollipop, which he'd begged for before the salesman had even measured his feet.

'You need one pair of shoes and one pair of winter boots,' Mom said, checking her list. 'And unless you get going we won't have time to get your winter boots today.'

There were at least a dozen open shoeboxes in front of Fudge, and the salesman – his name badge said *Mitch McCall* – kept checking his watch, like he was already late for some important appointment. Tootsie sat in her stroller, kicking her feet, or maybe she was admiring her new shoes. Finally, I said to Fudge, 'Why don't you just get the same shoes as me?'

'No thanks, Pete,' Fudge said. 'Your new shoes aren't that cool.'

'What do you mean?' I asked, looking down at my feet.

'I mean *cool*, Pete.'

'What's not cool about them?'

'Nothing's cool about them.'

Could he be right? I wondered. *Did I choose too fast just to be done with it? I do that sometimes. I can't help myself. I hate to shop. But are these shoes really that bad? Bad enough so the kids at school will laugh and say, 'Nice shoes, Hatcher.*

Where'd you find them, in the trash?' Should I try on another pair? Should I wait to see what Fudge chooses and then . . . Wait a minute, *I told myself. I can't believe I'm thinking this way, as if my five-year-old brother knows more about cool than me. Since when is he the expert on cool? Since when is he the expert on anything?*

'Make up your mind,' Mom told Fudge.

'I can't,' Fudge said. He was wearing one style on his right foot and another on his left. 'I have to have them both.'

'I'll count to twenty,' Mom said, 'while you decide.'

'I'm not deciding,' Fudge told her.

'You want me to decide for you?' Mom asked.

'No!'

Tootsie mimicked him. 'No!' Then she grabbed the yellow lollipop out of Fudge's hand and threw it. It hit Mitch McCall in the head, stuck to his hair, and hung there like

14

an ornament on a Christmas tree.

'Tootsie!' Mom cried. 'That wasn't polite.' But Tootsie laughed and clapped her sticky little hands anyway.

Mitch McCall grimaced as he pulled the lollipop off his head. It took some hairs with it, which really seemed to upset him, probably because he was already kind of bald on top.

'I'm so sorry,' Mom said, handing him a Wetwipe from her bag.

'Maybe you would prefer another salesperson,' Mitch McCall said, through teeth so tightly clenched his mouth hardly opened at all.

'No,' Mom said, 'you've been very helpful.'

'All right then,' Mitch McCall said, kneeling in front of Fudge. 'Let's get this over with. Make up your mind, son. There are other customers waiting.'

'I'm *not* your son,' Fudge told him.

15

'That's just a figure of speech,' Mom explained, quietly.

'A what?' Fudge asked.

'Never mind.' I could tell Mom was losing patience, too. 'Just choose your shoes, Fudge.'

Fudge pulled a couple of Fudge Bucks out of his pocket. He handed them to Mitch McCall. 'What's this?' Mitch asked.

'Money,' Fudge said. 'Enough for two pairs of shoes.'

'We don't take play money.'

'It's not play money,' Fudge told him. 'It's from the bank.'

'Bank?' Mitch McCall said. 'What bank?'

'The Farley Drexel Hatcher Bank.' I was surprised to hear Fudge use his whole name. Usually he throws a fit when someone tries to call him Farley Drexel instead of Fudge. 'It's a big bank,' he continued. 'It has zillions and trillions of Fudge Bucks.'

Mitch McCall turned to Mom. 'Harry's only accepts US currency and valid credit cards.'

Mom dug her wallet out of her purse. 'And I have my credit card right here,' she said, handing it to Mitch McCall. 'We'll take the black lace-ups with silver trim for Fudge and come back for his winter boots when you're less crowded.'

'Make it on a Wednesday,' Mitch McCall said. Then he muttered under his breath, 'That's my day off.'

'But, Mom—' Fudge started.

'That's it, Fudge,' Mom said. 'We're done shopping for shoes.'

'No fair!' Fudge cried.

'No feh!' Tootsie cried, as if she were Uncle Feather, repeating every word Fudge says.

'Let's go,' Mom said.

'I'm not going without all my shoes!' Fudge said. He folded his arms across his chest and

burrowed deeper into the chair.

Uh-oh, I thought, slowly backing away and out of the store. *This isn't looking good.* Outside, I pretended to check out the window displays. But I could see Mom trying to pull Fudge off his chair. When that didn't work, she tried to drag him by his feet. When *that* didn't work she gave up, went to the register, picked up her bags, and pushed Tootsie's stroller towards the door. She was probably thinking Fudge would follow. But she was wrong.

Suddenly he was whirling through the store like a tornado, destroying everything in his path. High heels flew off a display table. Baby shoes toppled from the shelves. Men's boots thumped to the floor. Mom chased Fudge and Mitch McCall chased Mom. As the rotating sock display crashed, Tootsie jumped up and down in her stroller, shrieking, as if her nutcase of a brother was putting on the best

18

show to hit Broadway in years.

I prayed no one from my class was at the store. No one who knows me or has ever known me. No one I might meet someday who would say, *Oh yeah, you're that kid with the weird brother who threw the fit at Harry's*. I backed away from the store windows and headed down the street, pretending I was just another guy strolling down Broadway – a guy from a perfectly normal family. I checked out the menu of the sushi restaurant two doors down from Harry's, browsed at the used-book table and flipped through magazines at the news-stand on the corner. Then I heard Mom calling my name. 'Peter, I could use some help here.' She was carrying Tootsie in one arm, struggling with the shopping bags in the other and still trying to push the stroller, which now held my screaming brother.

'You're too old for tantrums,' I shouted.

'If Mom didn't love *you*, you'd have a tantrum,' he cried.

'This has nothing to do with love,' Mom said, passing Tootsie to me, then trying to get Fudge out of the stroller.

'Yes, it does,' Fudge cried. 'If you really loved me you would have bought me both pairs of shoes!'

'You don't need two pairs of the same shoes,' Mom told him, as if she were talking to a reasonable person.

'They weren't the same.'

'They were close enough.'

'I wanted them,' Fudge whined.

'I know you did. But we can't buy everything you want.'

'Why?'

'We don't have the money to buy . . .' I could tell Mom was having a hard time explaining this. She thought for a minute before she

20

finished, '. . . just for the sake of buying. Money doesn't grow on trees.'

'I know it doesn't grow on trees,' Fudge said. 'You get it at the cash machine.'

'You can't just go to the cash machine whenever you want money,' Mom told him.

'Yes, you can,' Fudge said. 'You put in your card and money comes out. It works every time.'

'No. You have to *deposit* money into your account first,' Mom said. 'You work hard and try to save part of your salary every week. The cash machine is just a way to get some of your money out of your account. It doesn't spit out money because you want it. It's not that easy.'

'I know, Mom,' Fudge said. 'Sometimes you have to stand in line.'

Mom sighed and looked at me. 'Got any ideas, Peter?'

'Just tell him *no*! Stop trying to explain everything.'

Mom looked surprised. 'I never thought of that,' she said. 'I've always tried to explain things to my children.'

'Maybe that worked with me,' I said. 'But Fudge is another story.'

'Story?' Tootsie said.

'Not now,' Mom told her.

Tootsie started to cry. 'Story . . . now!'

When we got back to our building my best friend, Jimmy Fargo, was coming in with his father. They were loaded down with empty boxes.

'Have you told Peter the good news yet, Jimmy?' Mr Fargo asked.

'What good news?' I said.

'Oops,' Mr Fargo said. 'Guess I let the cat out of the bag.'

'You got a cat?' Fudge asked.

'Miaow?' Tootsie said. She has this animal alphabet book and every time she hears the

name of an animal she makes an animal sound.

Mr Fargo closed his eyes and shook his head. He always acts like he doesn't get it when he's around my family.

'I got new shoes,' Fudge told him.

'I see,' Mr Fargo said, trying to get a look at Fudge's feet over the boxes in his arms.

'No you don't,' Fudge told him, 'because my new shoes are in the bag.'

'Miaow?' Tootsie asked.

'We're not talking about cats,' Fudge told her. 'We're talking about shoes.'

Tootsie held up her foot. 'Sue,' she said. She hasn't learned to make the *sh* sound yet.

'Very nice,' Mr Fargo told her.

'Well . . .' Mom said to Mr Fargo, 'I have to get these kids upstairs for lunch.'

'And I have to get started on these boxes,' Mr Fargo told Mom.

23

'A new project?' Mom asked him.

'Oh yes,' Mr Fargo said. 'Very new.'

'I'll be right there,' Jimmy told his dad. 'I just have to talk to Peter.' Then he took my arm and led me outside.

'So what's up?' I asked.

'What do you mean?'

'You *know* what I mean. That *cat out of the bag* stuff.'

'Oh, that,' Jimmy said.

'Yeah, that.' Whatever it was, I could tell he didn't want to talk about it. So I changed the subject. 'You think these shoes are dorky?' I asked.

Jimmy checked them out. 'They look OK to me. Why?'

'Because . . .' I shook my head and stopped. I wasn't about to say, *Because Fudge said they were.* 'So what's the good news?' I asked again. He'd have to tell me sooner or later.

'You know my father's got a show coming up, right?' he said.

'Yeah.' Frank Fargo's an artist. And all of a sudden his paintings are starting to sell.

'So he needs a bigger place to paint,' Jimmy said.

'Yeah, so?'

'So he got this loft down in SoHo and . . .' Jimmy stopped and took a long look at my shoes. 'You know, maybe they are dorky. Where'd you get them?'

'Harry's.'

'Let's see the bottoms.'

I raised one foot to show Jimmy the bottom of my new shoe.

'I guess they're OK,' he said. 'Anyway, they won't take them back now, cause you already wore them in the street.'

'Could we get back to the *news*?'

'Oh, right, the news.' But he kept looking at

25

my shoes. 'How much were they?' he asked. 'I need new shoes before school starts.'

'I'll sell you these at a slight discount.'

'I don't think we wear the same size any more. Besides, if you think they're dorky, why would I want them?'

'They're not dorky.'

'Then how come you asked if I thought they were?'

'I'm done talking about these shoes, Jimmy, OK?'

'OK. Fine. Probably nobody will even notice them.'

'What do you mean?'

'Gotcha!' he said, sticking a finger in my gut and laughing. I hate when he does that.

I started back to our building. 'I'm going up for lunch.'

'Good idea,' Jimmy said. 'I'm starving. What are you having?'

'I don't know. Peanut butter, probably. So are you going to tell me or not?'

'Tell you what?'

'Whatever it is you don't want to tell me!'

'Oh, that . . .'

I waited while Jimmy looked up at the sky, then down at the ground, then back at the sky. Finally, he took a deep breath and said, 'I might as well get it over with because sooner or later you're going to find out anyway. Probably sooner since it's happening on Saturday.'

'What's happening on Saturday?'

'You know that artist's loft I told you about, where my dad's going to paint?'

'What about it?'

'We're going to live there.'

'What do you mean *live* there?'

'We're moving to SoHo on Saturday.'

'What do you mean *moving*?'

'Come on, Peter. You know what *moving* means.'

I kept shaking my head. It couldn't be true. It was just one of his jokes. Any second he'd poke me again and say *Gotcha*!

'But I'm still coming up here to go to school,' he said. 'So we'll still see each other every day.'

'What are you talking about? SoHo's like sixty or seventy blocks away.'

'I didn't say I was going to walk. I'm going to take the subway.'

'You're going to take the subway to school every day?' I asked. 'By yourself?'

'What's the big deal? Plenty of kids in seventh grade take the subway by themselves.'

I swallowed hard. I didn't know what the big deal was except I felt like I'd been punched in the gut for real and this time I felt like punching back. 'Why'd your father have to go and get a place way downtown?'

28

'That's where the lofts are. You have to be an artist to get one. Besides, our apartment is too small. It's always been too small.'

'You didn't used to think it was too small. One time you even invited me to move in.'

'We were younger then,' Jimmy said. 'I didn't know as much as I know now.'

'Just because your father's getting rich—' I began.

Jimmy didn't wait for me to finish. 'That's a really rude thing to say. He's not rich and you know it.'

'What's rude about having plenty of money?'

'He doesn't have plenty of money. He'll probably never have plenty of money.'

'Why are you acting like it's bad to have money?' I said.

'I don't know what it's like to have money, OK? All I know is my father got this loft

29

downtown and we're moving in. It's not like we're leaving the city the way you did.'

'That was just for one school year,' I argued. It's true we spent last year in New Jersey. In Princeton, to be exact. Because my parents wanted to check out living outside the city. It was OK. But when school ended we decided to come back. Jimmy was so glad we celebrated for a week. 'Besides,' I told him, 'I didn't have any choice about that.'

'You think I have a choice?' Jimmy asked. 'But to tell you the truth, I don't mind leaving.'

'Thanks a lot.'

'I'm not talking about leaving *you*,' Jimmy said. 'I'm talking about leaving an ant-sized apartment with no furniture. I'm tired of sleeping on a mat on the floor inches away from my father's face. I'm tired of smelling his salami and onion burps all night. I need my own space.'

I looked away.

'Are you trying to make me feel bad?' Jimmy asked. 'Because you're doing a pretty good job of it.'

I didn't answer. I couldn't.

'Look,' he said, 'you'll come down. We'll hang out. It'll be cool. Nothing's going to change.'

'What's wrong, Pete?' Fudge asked when I went upstairs for lunch.

'What do you mean?'

'You look like you just lost your best friend.'

'Where'd you learn that expression . . . from Grandma?' Grandma has an expression to fit every situation.

Fudge nodded. 'So, did you?'

'Did I *what*?'

'Lose your best friend?'

'I just found out Jimmy's moving down to SoHo.'

Mom put a peanut butter sandwich in front

of me. 'Frank Fargo told me. It's really good news for them, Peter.' She put an arm around my shoulder. 'I know it's going to be hard to say goodbye to Jimmy but—'

'I'm *not* saying goodbye to Jimmy! Didn't Mr Fargo tell you? He's still going to school with me. He's going to take the subway up here every day.'

'Is SoHo like Princeton?' Fudge asked.

'Princeton's in New Jersey, Turkey Brain.'

'SoHo is part of the city,' Mom told Fudge. 'You've been there.'

'So . . . ho ho ho,' Tootsie said, sounding like some miniature Santa.

Mom was impressed. 'That's right. SoHo.'

'I hate SoHo!' I shouted. Then I ran for my room and slammed the door and when I did, Tootsie started bawling.

'Thanks a lot, Pete,' Fudge called. 'Everybody was happy till you got home!'

3
Who's Mixed Up?

The minute Jimmy and his father moved out of our building, Henry started painting their apartment and fixing up the old kitchen. Lucky for the new people he did, because Frank Fargo never cleaned out his refrigerator. He kept everything until it turned green with mould and so smelly you nearly fell over when the door opened.

The new people have a kid Fudge's age. We met in the lobby the afternoon before school started. 'I'm Melissa Beth Miller and I'm in mixed-up group,' she announced. She had kid tattoos plastered up and down her arms.

'I'm in mixed-up group, too,' Fudge told her.

'It's not mixed-*up* group,' Mom said. 'It's mixed group.'

What does that mean? I wondered. *And how come this is the first I'm hearing about it?*

'That's a relief,' Melissa's mother said. 'We're new here and when we got Melissa's school assignment I was very concerned.'

By then, Tootsie had fallen asleep in her stroller. She was barefoot and Turtle started licking her toes. I don't know what it is about toes but all of a sudden he's an addict. It's like he can't help himself. Baby toes, old people's toes, clean toes, disgusting toes. As soon as he sees a set of toes he's at it – sniffing, nibbling, licking. I'm hoping he'll forget about toes once it's winter and nobody's walking around in sandals.

The second I let go of his leash to fish our mail out of the box, Turtle took off. By the time I looked up, he was across the lobby, sniffing Olivia Osterman's big toe. It was the only

one sticking out of her open-toed shoe. Mrs Osterman spends a lot of time in the lobby, sitting on the leather sofa, watching people come and go. She's lived in our building longer than anyone – more than sixty years. She's close to ninety now. When she was younger she was a Broadway star. Grandma saw her perform. She still dresses up every day, wearing big hats and lots of jewellery. Everyone in the building knows her and stops to talk. She hands out little boxes of raisins to the kids, as if every day were Hallowe'en. She carries dog biscuits, too, so all the dogs in the building are her friends.

The only problem is, she doesn't get why I named my dog Turtle. I've explained a million times that I had a tiny pet turtle and when my brother was three he swallowed him. So when I got a dog, I named him after my turtle. It makes perfect sense to everyone but Mrs Osterman. 'A turtle is a turtle,' she says. 'A dog is a dog.

Would you name your cat *Monkey*, or your monkey *Kangaroo*?' I never know how to answer that question.

I was so busy thinking about Mrs Osterman I didn't notice Mom, who was chasing half a dozen apples that had tumbled out of our grocery bag. Sometimes Mom tells me I'm just like Dad, that I don't notice what's going on right under my nose.

By then, Fudge and Melissa were racing around the lobby, laughing and screaming.

'Fudge,' Mom called. 'You know you're not supposed to run in the lobby.'

'Melissa,' Mrs Miller called, 'come over here, please.'

Mom laughed. 'Welcome to our building,' she said to Mrs Miller. 'It's not always this chaotic.'

Right, I thought, *sometimes it's worse.*

When Fudge came back and heard Mrs Miller telling Mom she worked at the Social Services

programme at Roosevelt Hospital, he asked, 'How much do you make?'

'Excuse me?' Mrs Miller said, as if she couldn't possibly have heard what she thought she heard.

'Fudge,' Mom said, 'that's not a polite question.' She shook her head at Mrs Miller. 'My son isn't usually so rude.'

Oh yeah, he is, I thought.

'I don't get why grown-ups don't like to talk about money,' Fudge said to Melissa.

'Because they're grown-ups,' Melissa said. 'That's why.'

Mom and Mrs Miller half-laughed the way parents do when they're embarrassed but don't want to admit it. Then they exchanged business cards. 'I'm a dental hygienist,' Mom said.

'We could use a good dentist,' Mrs Miller said, reading Mom's card aloud. '*Dr Martha Julie*.'

'The dentist with two first names,' Fudge

sang, hopping around Melissa. 'You get to watch videos while she's checking your teeth.'

'Which ones?' Melissa asked.

'Whichever ones you want. But she doesn't like it when you laugh hard, so don't bring anything too funny.'

'Funny is the best,' Melissa said.

'I know,' Fudge agreed.

'I'll call to set up an appointment,' Mrs Miller told Mom.

'I'm there Tuesdays, Fridays and every other Saturday,' Mom said. She picked up our grocery bags. 'See you soon.'

As I pushed Tootsie in her stroller, Mom tried to guide Fudge towards the elevator but he pulled back. 'Guess what?' he called to Melissa. 'Pete's best friend lived in your apartment. They didn't have any beds.'

'That's because his father thought it was better to sleep on the floor,' I said. I don't know why I

38

thought I had to defend Frank Fargo, but I did.

'I have a bed,' Melissa said. 'Want to see it?' she asked.

'Can I, Mom?' Fudge said.

'Some other time,' Mom said. 'We have a lot to do to get ready for school.'

Melissa walked us to the elevator. 'See you in mixed-up group,' she told Fudge.

'Mixed-up group for mixed-up kids!' Fudge sang, giving her a high five.

All through dinner I wondered if Fudge was really going into a class for mixed-up kids. Later, while Mom was getting Tootsie ready for bed, I decided to find out. 'So what's with this mixed-up group thing?'

'It's called *mixed group*,' Mom told me.

'Look, Mom, if he's repeating kindergarten you can tell me. I won't let the cat out of the bag.'

'Miaow,' Tootsie said, as Mom changed her diaper.

'He's *not* repeating kindergarten,' Mom said. 'You know he's very smart.'

'But he says his class is for *mixed-up* kids.'

'I can't imagine where he got that idea,' Mom said, looking at me. 'Peter, you didn't suggest—'

'No way, Mom.'

'Because this is an accelerated programme. All the children are ready to read and write. They're just not old enough for official first grade. You know how smart Fudge is. You know he's very mature for his age.'

I laughed. So did Tootsie, even though she didn't have a clue what we were talking about.

'He is, Peter!'

'Sure, Mom. If you say so.'

'His self-esteem is at stake here. He should be proud to be in mixed group.'

'I don't think you have to worry about his self-esteem. He thinks he's the greatest.'

'Not if he's got the idea he's going into a class for mixed-up children.'

'What happens if he gets another Rat Face?' I asked. Rat Face was his kindergarten teacher last year, when we lived in Princeton. When she refused to call him Fudge he kicked her. In less than an hour he had to be transferred to another class.

'I've met the teaching team and they seem very nice. Fudge will be in William's section. This is his third year with mixed group. So he has some experience.'

'Nobody has enough experience for Fudge,' I said.

'Let's try to have a positive attitude, Peter. OK?'

'I am positive.' *Positive it'll be a disaster, just like it always is with Fudge.*

41

4
Richie Richest

I admit I was worried about my first day of seventh grade. I wondered if I'd be considered a *new* kid, because I wasn't there last year to start middle school with everyone else. But how can you be a *new* kid when you've only missed one year? I'd be more like a new *old* kid, wouldn't I? I mean, I wouldn't know everyone at middle school but I'd know all the kids who'd been in fifth grade with me. And I'd still have the same best friend.

Fudge didn't seem at all worried about starting a new school. He and Melissa skipped all the way there. I wish Jimmy still lived in our building so we could walk to school together. Instead I walked with Sheila Tubman. Not that

42

I wanted to but what choice did I have? We went down in the elevator together. It would have been rude to cross the street just to avoid her, right? I was still hoping we wouldn't be in the same homeroom or any of the same classes.

The bad news is, Sheila's in my homeroom. She's in my science class and Spanish, too. But I'm trying to keep a positive attitude, like Mom said. The good news is, Jimmy's also in my homeroom and better yet, in my humanities section. We even have the same lunch period. And nobody at school acted like I was a new kid. Most kids either didn't remember I lived someplace else last year, or didn't care.

After school Jimmy came over, same as always. I told him about Melissa and her mother and how Henry painted the apartment and fixed up the kitchen. 'They got a new refrigerator,' I said, expecting Jimmy to laugh

and make some joke about salami and onion sandwiches. But he didn't.

We hung out in the park for a while – at the top of our special rock – then, just like that, Jimmy said he had to go home. I forgot for a minute he'd moved, that he lived downtown now, that he had to take the subway home by himself. I walked him to Central Park West and Seventy-second Street.

Jimmy and I have been best friends since third grade. He lived around the corner then. It was the first place in the city I was allowed to walk to by myself. I really liked Jimmy's mom. She told me to call her Anita, not Mrs Fargo. We had this special game. Every time I left her house she gave me a graham cracker, in case I got hungry on the way home. That was a big joke since it took about two minutes to get to my building. I was so mad at her when she took off for Vermont, leaving Jimmy with his dad.

But then I was happy when Jimmy and his dad moved into our building. Then I was mad at her again, because Jimmy was.

Jimmy still doesn't like to talk about the divorce or his mother. He keeps everything to himself. He visits her at Christmas and for a month in the summer. I hope I never see her again because if I do, I'll tell her exactly what I think about what she did to Jimmy. And don't tell me there are two sides to every story, like Mom does, because I've seen Jimmy's side up close. Not that I want him to move to Vermont. That would be a lot worse than SoHo. I'd never get to see him then. Now I know how he felt when I left the city last year.

I watched as Jimmy disappeared down the stairs into the station. I wonder when Mom and Dad will let me take the subway to SoHo on my own?

*

That night at dinner, Fudge went on and on about his first day of school. 'I have two teachers in my room, William and Polly. And a library helper. That makes three.'

'You need three teachers,' I said, 'maybe more.'

'Because I'm smart, right?'

'Oh yeah, they don't come any smarter than you.'

'How many teachers do you have, Pete?'

'A different one every hour.'

'Wow . . . you're *really* smart.'

Dad said, 'When you're in seventh grade you'll have as many teachers as Peter.'

'My library helper comes two times every week,' Fudge said. 'He's seventeen. Next year he's going to college. Know what his name is? Jonathan Girdle.'

I laughed and said, 'You probably got that wrong, Turkey Brain.'

46

'Peter!' Mom said. 'What did we discuss last night?'

'Uh . . . I don't know.'

'Self-esteem,' Mom said. 'Don't you remember?'

'What's that got to do with . . .' I stopped before I finished. Was she talking about me calling Fudge *Turkey Brain*? Mom nodded like she could read my mind.

But Fudge didn't pay any attention. He went on as if he were the only one at the table. 'Jonathan told us some people think his name is funny, so I told him some people think *my* name is funny. Then this girl named Rebecca Noodle said a lot of people think *her* name is funny. Then Pluto Stevenson said *everybody* thinks his name is funny.'

'*Pluto?*' I said.

'Yes, Pluto. But he's not my new best friend. My new best friend is—'

'Wait a minute,' I said, interrupting. 'One day of school and you have a new best friend?'

'Yeah, Pete. I do.'

I have to hand it to Fudge. He always manages to find a friend. He never worries like I do, when I go someplace new, that maybe no one will like him. 'Guess what my new best friend's name is?' Fudge asked later that night. I was at my desk. I'd just finished my math homework and was about to start on Spanish. We're having a vocabulary quiz on Friday.

'I'm doing my homework,' I told him. 'You're not supposed to bother me while I'm studying. And you're supposed to knock if my door is closed.' Fudge and I each have half a bedroom. There's a divider wall with shelves between us. But we have our own doors to the hallway.

'I brought you a rice cake,' Fudge said in his

best-little-boy-in-the-world voice. He held it out
to me.

He's the one who loves rice cakes, not
me. They make me gag. They're like eating
cardboard. 'I don't want a rice cake,' I told him.
'You know how I feel about rice cakes. Anyway,
aren't you supposed to be in bed?'

'I can't go to bed until you guess,' he said,
nibbling at the rice cake himself.

'OK, what am I supposed to guess this time?'

'Pay attention, Pete!' he said. 'You're
supposed to guess my new friend's name.'

'If you want me to guess, you have to give
me a clue,' I told him.

'OK . . . his first name is what I want to be
when I grow up.'

'King?' I guessed.

'Wrong!'

'President?'

'Very funny, Pete. Try again.'

'Let's see . . .' I pretended to think about it. 'Oh, I've got it. *Miser?*'

'No!' He shoved half the rice cake into his mouth at once. 'It's Rich.' He waited for my reaction. When I didn't say anything he repeated, 'His name is *Rich*. Get it, Pete? It's what I want to be when I grow up!' When I still didn't say anything, he added, 'We call him Richie. And his last name is even better. Here's a clue. He's related to someone very famous. Someone we know.' He stuffed the rest of the rice cake into his mouth and brushed off his hands. The crumbs landed on my *Living Spanish* textbook.

'I don't know anyone really famous.'

'Yes you do.'

'I give up.'

Fudge whispered in my ear. 'He's *You-Know-Who*'s cousin.'

'We've been through this before,' I told him,

50

wiping off my ear. 'Harry Potter isn't real. He's
a—'

But before I could finish Fudge spat on the
back of his hand three times. 'You said his
name out loud! You have to spit three times
or something terrible will happen. Hurry!' He
spat on the back of his other hand. I don't know
why Fudge thinks you're not supposed to say
the name Harry Potter out loud, but he does. It's
some kind of magic he invented. I knew he was
too young to listen to the book on tape but Mom
and Dad played it anyway, driving back from
summer vacation. To tell the truth, it's easier to
spit than argue with him. So I did. Three times
on the back of my hand.

'Whew,' Fudge said. 'That was a close one.'

'I hate to break it to you,' I told him, 'but
Potter's a common name. I know at least two
kids at school whose last name is Potter. It
doesn't mean anything.'

'You are so wrong, Pete!'

Uncle Feather agreed with Fudge. 'You are so wrong, Pete . . . so wrong, wrong, wrong.'

'Cover Bird Brain's cage, will you?' I said. 'I can't concentrate on my homework with him yakking.'

'Yak, yak, yak,' Uncle Feather said.

I reached for my headset and turned up the volume. Sometimes I wonder how I ever survived without it.

Richie Potter was at our apartment when I got home from school the next day. He's two heads taller than Fudge and so thin you can count his ribs through his shirt. He has a brush cut, and big eyes that blink a lot, like maybe he needs glasses. I could see why Fudge got the idea he was You-Know-Who's cousin.

He started wheezing right away. 'Allergies,' he explained, digging his inhaler out of his

52

backpack and puffing twice. 'You must have dust mites.'

'I don't know,' Fudge said. 'But Pete has a dog.'

'Dogs are OK as long as they don't lick me,' Richie said. 'If they lick me I get hives.'

'What about brothers?' Fudge asked.

'Brothers are OK unless they lick their dogs.' He and Fudge started laughing. 'Does your brother lick his dog?'

'Maybe,' Fudge said. 'Hey, Pete, do you—'

'No!' I said.

Fudge and Richie laughed themselves silly.

'Want to see my bird?' Fudge asked. 'He can talk.' Richie followed Fudge and I followed Richie. I like to be around when Fudge introduces his bird to a new friend. 'Presenting . . .' Fudge said with a flourish, 'the *one* . . . the *only* . . . Uncle Feather!'

'I have an Uncle Jocko,' Richie said.

'Is your Uncle Jocko a bird?' Fudge asked.

'No,' Richie said. 'He's my mother's brother.'

'Uncle Feather's not related to my mother or my father,' Fudge said. 'He's just related to me. He's all mine.'

'So, what does he say?' Richie asked.

'Whatever you want him to say.'

Richie thought about it. Then he said, 'Zoopideezop.'

Uncle Feather just stood there, his head cocked to one side.

'Try something else,' Fudge said. 'He likes real words. Especially *bad* words.'

So Richie said all the bad words he knew but Uncle Feather wasn't impressed.

'You try,' Richie told Fudge.

'What's up?' Fudge asked Uncle Feather.

Usually Uncle Feather answers, 'Whassup . . . whassup . . . whassup.' But this time, nothing.

'What's wrong?' I asked Uncle Feather. 'Cat

54

got your tongue?' I wouldn't say that in front of Tootsie or she'd start miaowing. But Tootsie was taking her afternoon nap.

'Don't tease him, Pete!'

'I'm not teasing him. I'm trying to get him to talk.'

'He's not in the mood,' Fudge said. 'Come on, Richie, let's get a snack.'

I followed them to the kitchen. Mom was still in her whites from work.

'Are you a doctor?' Richie asked.

'No,' Mom said, 'a dental hygienist.'

'One of my grandpas is a very famous neurosurgeon,' Richie said. 'He fixes brains.'

'We know this girl who fell off her bike,' Fudge said, 'and her brains came out her ears.'

'My grandpa could have put them back in,' said Richie.

'Too bad she didn't know your grandpa,' Fudge said.

'What's he talking about?' I asked Mom.

Mom shrugged and rolled her eyes as if she was wondering the same thing. Then she said, 'Would you boys like a snack?'

'Yes, please,' Richie answered. 'I'll have broccoli.'

'Broccoli,' Mom repeated.

'Yes, please,' Richie said. 'I'd like lightly steamed florets.'

Mom seemed really surprised. 'I don't think we have any broccoli in the house, but we do have carrots.'

'Carrots are good,' Richie said. 'Dipped in either hummus or tahini.'

Now Mom was really surprised. 'We don't have hummus or tahini. But we have peanut butter and that tastes a lot like tahini.'

'Don't you have a cook?' Richie asked.

'No, I'm afraid we don't,' Mom said.

56

'Oh, I'm sorry,' Richie said. 'I didn't know you were poor.'

'We're hardly poor,' Mom said, serving him a bowl of baby carrots with some peanut butter. 'We just don't have a cook.'

Fudge watched as Richie took a carrot and swirled it in peanut butter. 'Can I have peanut butter and banana?' he asked Mom.

'You know where the bananas are,' she told him, pouring them each a glass of milk. 'You can help yourself.'

'Carrots are hard to eat with loose teeth,' Richie told Fudge, as he wiggled his front top tooth. 'Soon I'll look like you.'

'What do you mean?' Fudge asked.

Richie pointed to his mouth. 'No teeth on top.'

That's when it dawned on me that Fudge's classmates are finally catching up with him. They're losing their teeth.

'Know how much I got from the tooth fairy

when I lost my first tooth?' Richie asked.

'How much?' Fudge said.

'Twenty dollars. And that was just from the tooth fairy. My grandma gave me another twenty and my twin uncles gave me twenty apiece.'

Eighty dollars a tooth! I was thinking.

'How much did I get, Mom?' Fudge asked.

'Well, Fudge,' Mom began, 'you didn't lose your teeth in the usual way.'

'How'd he lose them?' Richie asked.

'He was trying to fly off the top of the climbing bars,' I said.

'Fly?' Richie asked.

'He was only three,' Mom explained.

'So what happened?' Richie asked.

'What do you think?' I answered. 'He crash-landed and knocked out his top front teeth.'

'But I didn't lose them,' Fudge said. 'I swallowed them.'

'At least that's what we *think* happened,'

Mom said. 'We're really not sure.'

'So no tooth fairy came?' Richie asked.

'Mom,' Fudge began, 'how come the tooth fairy—'

Mom answered quickly. 'You were so young when you lost your teeth the tooth fairy put your money in the bank.'

I gave Mom a look. She shot me one right back.

'So that means I have money in the bank?' Fudge asked.

'You certainly do.'

'How much?'

'Let's talk about it later,' Mom said.

'My mom doesn't like to talk about money,' Fudge told Richie.

'My mom loves to talk about money,' Richie said, sporting a milk moustache. 'She's a designer. You can get clothes with her name on them. She's very famous. So's my father. He builds office

buildings. And my grandma's filthy rich.'

'You mean from counting her money?' Fudge asked.

'I don't know,' Richie said. 'Maybe.'

'She should take her money to the bank and get it washed,' Fudge told him.

'That's a good idea.' Richie bit into a carrot with his back teeth.

'I have a lot of good ideas,' Fudge said.

'I know,' Richie said. 'That's why I want to be your friend.'

The next day Richie *Richest* was back. 'So, where's the toy room?'

'What toy room?' Fudge asked.

'You know,' Richie said, 'the room where you keep all your toys.'

'I keep my toys in *my* room.'

'That's it? That's all the toys you have?'

'He has more than he needs,' Mom told

Richie. She was getting Tootsie up from her nap.

Richie shook his head. 'I can have any toy I want whenever I want it.'

'Even Lego Panorama?' Fudge asked.

Richie shrugged. 'Whatever.'

'Did you hear that?' Fudge said. 'He can have any toy he wants whenever he wants it.'

'Yes,' Mom said and she took a deep breath. 'I certainly did hear that.'

'But I'm not spoiled,' Richie said. 'There's a difference between having everything you want and being spoiled.'

'Is there, Mom?' Fudge asked.

'I suppose it's possible,' Mom said.

'We have a house at the beach,' Richie announced. 'Do you?'

'No, we don't,' Mom said.

'Our house is on the ocean side but we keep our boat in the bay. I have two half-brothers who are also rich and famous. You've probably

heard of them, Jeffrey and Colin Potter. They make movies.'

'Pete,' Fudge said, 'if I cut you in half then I'd have a half-brother! And Tootsie could have the other half.'

'That's not exactly what a half-brother is,' I told him.

'Jeffrey and Colin are from my father's first marriage,' Richie told Fudge. 'After his divorce he married my mother and they had me. My mother is twenty years younger than my father. She says I'm very smart. And extremely handsome. Do you think I'm handsome?'

The kid was on a roll. There was no stopping him now.

'Why, yes,' Mom said, 'you and Fudge are both handsome.'

'Which of us is more handsome?' Richie asked.

'I wouldn't want to have to choose,' Mom said.

'What is this, a beauty contest?' I asked.

That got Fudge and Richie laughing so hard Richie had to dig out his inhaler and take a couple of puffs.

That night at dinner Mom told Dad, 'Fudge has an interesting new friend.'

'Interesting friends are better than boring ones,' Dad said.

We were having pasta primavera – that's spaghetti with a bunch of vegetables on top.

I asked Mom if I could have my pasta with just plain tomato sauce but Mom said, 'Vegetables are very important.'

'Richie Potter likes broccoli,' Fudge said.

'We know,' I told him.

'It makes his pee smell funny.'

'Fudge,' Mom said, 'we don't talk about what we do in the bathroom at mealtimes.'

'Why not?' Fudge asked.

'Anyway, it's asparagus that makes pee smell funny,' I told him, 'not broccoli.'

'Peter . . .' Dad warned.

'Broccoli too,' Fudge said. 'I know because he let me smell it.'

'That's *enough*, boys,' Dad said, which got Tootsie going.

'Eeee . . . eee . . . eee,' she shrieked.

'Fudge's new friend brags about everything,' I said.

'He even brags about his poops,' Fudge told us.

'I'm not surprised,' I said.

'But Pete, if you saw what he made you'd understand. It was thiiiiis long.' Fudge held out his hands showing me exactly *how* long.

'That's it!' Mom said. 'I don't want to hear another inappropriate word at this meal.'

5
Bye-bye, Sue!

Jimmy asked me to come down to see his new place. I convinced Dad to take me on Saturday afternoon. The downside was, we had to bring Fudge and Tootsie with us because Mom was at work. She says her new job with Dr Julie is the best she's ever had.

As soon as we were through the turnstile at the subway station, a train came along. We got lucky and found seats together. Sometimes the subway cars are so crowded you have to stand squeezed between strangers – *like sardines in a can*, as Grandma would say. Personally, I hate the idea of being compared to a sardine. The smell reminds me of cat food, even though Grandma says sardines are good for your

bones. Probably cat food is, too.

It wasn't until we got off the subway at Spring Street that I noticed Fudge was wearing just one shoe. On his other foot he had on only his yellow and black striped bumblebee sock. 'Where's your shoe?' I asked him.

'What shoe?'

'The one that's *not* on your foot.'

'Oh, that shoe.'

Dad said, 'Put on your other shoe, Fudge.'

'I can't.'

'Why not?' Dad asked.

'I took it off to itch my foot and now it's gone.'

'Gone?' Dad said.

'Yes,' Fudge said.

'That was one of your new shoes,' Dad told him.

'I *know*, Dad.'

'And now you've lost it.'

'I didn't *lose* it. I *know* where it is. It's on the subway.'

'The subway?' Dad said.

'Yes,' Fudge said.

I should have convinced Dad to let me take the subway to Jimmy's on my own. There's no such thing as a simple trip downtown with my brother. He turns everything into a major production.

Dad spotted a transit cop and waved her over, calling, 'Excuse me . . .'

'Can I help you?' the transit cop asked.

'Yes,' Dad said. 'I'd like to report a missing shoe.'

She looked surprised. 'A missing shoe?'

'That's right,' Dad told her. 'Fudge, show the policewoman your shoe.'

'How can I show it to her if it's missing?' Fudge asked.

'Show her the shoe that's *not* missing.' Dad was definitely losing patience.

67

'Ohhh, *that* shoe.' Fudge held up his foot.

The transit cop whipped out a small notebook and jotted down all the information. 'Black with silver trim, child's size. Lost on the A train on Saturday, September 14.' She looked at Dad. 'What time would you say?'

'Somewhere between 2:00 and 2:30 p.m.,' Dad told her. 'Somewhere between Seventy-second Street and here.'

When she was done taking notes she closed her notebook and shoved it into her pocket. 'We'll do our best but I wouldn't count on getting it back.'

'I have to get it back,' Fudge said. 'I need it for school.'

The cop shrugged.

'I told Mom I needed two pairs but she wouldn't listen.'

'I don't blame her,' the cop said, 'with what shoes cost nowadays.'

68

'I have plenty of money.' He pulled a wad of Fudge Bucks out of his pocket and waved it around.

'You keep those for an emergency,' the cop told him.

'This *is* an emergency,' Fudge said.

'You want my advice? Next time, keep on both your shoes.'

'Even if my foot itches?'

'Especially then,' the cop said. 'Otherwise, you're going to be kissing more than one shoe goodbye.'

'Bye-bye, sue!' Tootsie sang, blowing kisses.

The transit cop did a double take. 'How does she know my name?'

'Your name is *Shoe*?' Fudge asked.

'No, it's Sue!'

No way was I going to tell the cop my sister can't pronounce the *sh* sound.

*

Finally, *finally*, I got to Jimmy's. The streets in SoHo are narrow and paved with cobblestones. It's a really old part of the city. The buildings used to be factories but now most of them have stores or art galleries on the first floor and lofts upstairs. Dad said he'd be back for me in an hour and a half. I told him to take his time.

The Fargos' loft is a huge open space, with an old wooden floor and a pressed tin ceiling. 'Pretty cool, huh?' Jimmy asked. 'You know how many windows we have? Sixteen. Want to count them?'

'I believe you,' I said. They were gigantic floor-to ceiling windows.

'Know how high the ceiling is?' Jimmy asked. He didn't wait for me to guess. 'Sixteen feet. Want to measure it yourself?'

'That's OK. I can see it's really high.' I looked around. 'You could set up a bowling alley in here,' I told him.

'Yeah,' Jimmy said. 'Or a basketball court.'

'You could blade.'

'Or flood it and play ice hockey,' Jimmy said.

'Ice hockey?'

'Gotcha!' he said, laughing and sticking a finger in my gut.

'I hate when you do that,' I told him.

'I know, that's why I do it. Come on, I'll show you around.'

There wasn't much to see. Frank Fargo's canvases were stacked against one wall. There were two paint-splattered worktables. Old coffee cans held brushes. It smelled good, like the art room at school. There was no regular furniture, but that was no surprise, since they didn't have any before either. At the opposite end of the loft was a kitchen. There were no doors anywhere, except for the bathroom.

'And right about here,' Jimmy said, standing in front of an *X* that had been chalked on the

floor, 'we're going to build two bedrooms, one for me, and the other for my dad and . . .' He stopped for a minute to look out the window. Then he looked back at the floor. 'Oh yeah, and we're adding another bathroom, so we don't have to share.'

I wouldn't mind having a bathroom all to myself instead of sharing with Fudge and Tootsie. At least Fudge uses the toilet. Not that he remembers to flush half the time, but it's better than a potty. Not that Tootsie actually uses her potty for anything except a place to sit, but someday she will and then . . .

'And I'm getting a bunk bed,' Jimmy said, 'so you can stay over. We might get a dog, too.'

'A dog?' I was surprised. Mr Fargo's never really liked Turtle and Turtle isn't crazy about Mr Fargo either. 'What kind of dog?'

'A Yorkie, I think.'

'A Yorkie? But they're so small.'

'I know.'

I tried to imagine Jimmy and his father with a Yorkie but I couldn't.

'So how about a game of sock hockey?' Jimmy asked.

Sock hockey's a game we invented. 'Yeah, sure,' I told him, kicking off my shoes. Jimmy passed me a broom, grabbed another for himself, threw down a box of Jell-O for the puck, and the game began. We've never had such a great place to play. You could run and slide from one end of the loft to the other without worrying about knocking over lamps or furniture, not just because there weren't any, but because the place was so big.

We were totally into our game when we heard banging on the door. 'Uh-oh . . .' Jimmy said. He wiped his sweaty face with the bottom of his T-shirt and went to the door. 'Who is it?' he called.

'This is Goren, your downstairs neighbour.'
He spoke slowly, in an accent I couldn't place.

'Don't open it,' I whispered.

'But Goren *is* our downstairs neighbour,'
Jimmy said. 'I met him this morning.'

I shook my head. 'Don't unlock the door.'

'My dad will be back in a few minutes,' Jimmy
called through the locked door. Actually, he
had no idea when Frank Fargo would be home.

'So what's going on?' Goren asked from the
other side of the door. 'All that pounding – it
sounds like the ceiling's going to cave in. How
am I supposed to concentrate?'

'Uh . . . sorry,' Jimmy said. 'We were just
uh . . .'

'Moving stuff around,' I called, finishing for
him.

'Oh,' Goren said. 'I thought maybe you were
playing sock hockey.'

Jimmy and I looked at each other. If we

invented the game, how could this guy possibly know about it? 'We'll try to be more careful with our . . . uh . . . cartons,' Jimmy told him.

'Fair enough,' Goren said. 'And I'll try to get back to work.'

When he was gone Jimmy let out a *whew* . . . and we put away the brooms.

By the time we got back from SoHo Mom was home. 'How was your day?' she asked.

'Very nice,' Dad told her. 'We had a good time, didn't we, boys?'

'I had fun at Jimmy's,' I said.

'And I had fun on the subway,' Fudge told her. 'So did Tootsie.'

'I guess that makes it unanimous,' Mom said, 'because I had a good day at work.'

'Yay . . . it's unanimous!' Fudge sang.

That's when Mom looked down and noticed that Fudge was wearing one shoe and one

fringed and beaded moccasin. 'Where did you get that moccasin?' she asked.

'From the store,' Fudge said. 'The man took it out of the window. It was a real bargain. Right, Dad?'

Dad nodded.

'But where's your other shoe, Fudgie?' Mom said.

Fudge didn't answer.

Dad put his arm around Mom's shoulder. 'It's a long story, honey.'

'Reaallly long!' Fudge added, laughing.

The next day, when the transit police still hadn't found the missing shoe, Mom went back to Harry's, this time without Fudge. She bought another pair of shoes, the exact same ones he got the first time. So in case Fudge grows a third foot he'll be all set. And with my brother, nothing is impossible!

76

6

Mr Money

Instead of taking picture books to bed, the way he used to, Fudge is thumbing through catalogues. He's choosing presents for Christmas and birthdays. He's working so far ahead he's already circled what he wants when he's twelve. Underwater watches, home entertainment systems with huge TV screens, digital cameras, telescopes so powerful you can see Venus, a water trampoline bigger than his room and mine put together.

'Look at this, Pete,' he said one night.

It was a rope bridge, forty feet long. It cost thousands of dollars. 'That'd be useful,' I told him.

'I know,' he said. 'Uncle Feather would really like it.'

Lucky for us Fudge doesn't know how to go online.

The first time Fudge went to Richie Potter's for a play date, he came home full of ideas. 'We need a bigger apartment.'

'A bigger apartment would be nice,' Mom said, 'but we're very lucky we have what we do.'

'But Mom, I need two rooms. One for me and one for my toys,' Fudge said. 'If you and Dad slept in the living room, I could sleep in your room and keep my toys in *my* room.'

'Keep dreaming, Fudge!' I said.

'I'm not dreaming, Pete. I'm wide awake.'

Later he came to my room. I was instant messaging with Jimmy Fargo when I was supposed to be making a journal entry for humanities. I'd be in big trouble if Mom or Dad knew. The computer goes back in the living

room if I don't keep up my grades.

'The problem with our family is,' Fudge said, 'we don't have enough money. We need to get more. And fast.'

'Cheer up,' I said, 'maybe we'll win the lottery.'

His eyes lit up. 'The lottery! That's it.'

But when he told Dad his brilliant idea, Dad said, 'Buying lottery tickets is just a way to waste money.'

'No,' Fudge argued. 'It's a way to get rich fast!'

'Fudge,' Mom said, 'we're happy the way we are. We're grateful for all the good things we have. Like each other and our health and—'

'That's *you*,' Fudge said. 'Not *me*!'

'This is getting out of hand,' Mom said to Dad.

'I'm inclined to agree,' Dad said.

*

By the third week of school Fudge had homework. I don't remember ever having homework in kindergarten, or even in first grade. He was working on the floor, in front of the TV, while Mom and Dad watched the evening news. 'Let me see that,' I said, grabbing his paper.

Fill in the Blanks

I really like _____.

_____ is good.

_____ is fun.

I dream about _____.

I like to read about _____.

I like to draw _____.

A good name for me is _____.

'How's he supposed to fill in the blanks when he can't even write?' I asked my parents.

'I can write,' Fudge said.

'Yeah, three words.'

'I don't need more than that,' he told me, grabbing back his paper.

He whipped right through it, saying, 'This is so easy.' Then he proudly handed his paper back to me.

Fill in the Blanks

I really like _money_.

money is good.

money is fun.

I dream about _money_.

I like to read about _money_.

I like to draw _money_.

A good name for me is _Mr money_.

Two days later Fudge was sent to the school counsellor to be evaluated.

'It was so fun,' he told us that night. 'We played games and drew pictures. Guess what I drew?' He didn't wait for us to guess. 'Money,

money, money. And I made dollar signs with wings. Lots and lots of them.'

'Mun-eeee,' Tootsie sang.

Mom and Dad got a call from the school counsellor, who asked to meet with them. They went on Wednesday afternoon. Grandma babysat for Tootsie. When they got back Mom was really upset. 'Do you know what the counsellor asked us?' Mom said to Grandma. 'She asked if we're having a problem at home. If we've lost our jobs or need financial help. It was so embarrassing.'

Grandma made Mom a cup of tea. 'You can't take it personally, Anne,' Grandma said. 'She's just doing her job.'

'That's not all,' Mom continued. 'She suggested that instead of *buying* things for our children we could stress all the good things in life that are free. As if we don't.' Mom choked up. 'I just don't know what to do about this.'

'It'll pass, honey,' Grandma said.

'What if it doesn't?' Mom asked.

'Let's not worry about that before we have to,' Grandma said.

That night, when Mom came to my room to say goodnight, she sat on the edge of my bed. 'Peter, I've been wondering . . . have Dad and I taught you that the best things in life are free, like good health and love and friendship? That's what we stress in our family, isn't it?'

'Yeah, Mom, sure.'

'And you understand that no matter how much money you have you aren't necessarily happy? You know that, don't you, Peter?'

'Sure, Mom. I know that. It's like no matter how much money Jimmy might have he can't make his parents get back together. He can't even make them like each other.'

Mom got teary-eyed.

'But just so you know, Mom, I don't think about that stuff every day.'

'Don't think about what?'

'It's not like I get up in the morning and say to myself, *Wow, the best things in life are free!*'

'What do you think about?'

'First thing in the morning, you mean?'

Mom nodded.

'I don't know. Usually I wish I could sleep later. Or I wonder if I studied enough for the Spanish test. Or I think about the Mets or the Knicks or the Rangers, depending on the season.'

'But you don't get up in the morning and think about money, do you?'

'No, Mom. I mean, maybe if we were seriously deprived and we didn't have enough to eat . . . but then I guess I'd wake up thinking about food, not money.'

'Just so long as money isn't number one in

84

your thoughts,' Mom said. 'Or even number twenty.'

'Probably if I made a list, it wouldn't be,' I told her.

'Thank you, Peter. That makes me feel much better.'

7
The Green Stuff

It was Grandma's idea to take Fudge to Washington, D.C., to the Bureau of Printing and Engraving. 'Let him see the green stuff hot off the press,' she said to Dad, while the two of them were doing the dinner dishes.

'What green stuff?' Fudge asked. They thought he was safely tucked away in bed but I'd seen him crawl under the kitchen table, where he was listening to every word.

'Fudge, what are you doing under the table?' Mom asked on her way back from putting Tootsie to sleep. 'You're supposed to be in bed.'

'I can't go to bed until I know about the green stuff.'

'What green stuff?' Mom asked.

'I don't know,' Fudge said. 'That's what I'm trying to find out.'

'The green stuff is money,' Grandma explained.

'Oh, money,' Fudge said. 'I *love* money!'

'We know,' I told him.

'Are you going to cook some money?' he asked Grandma, laughing.

Grandma laughed with him and shook her head. 'You don't *cook* it. The government *prints* it.'

'I can print,' Fudge said. 'I can print the whole alphabet.'

'We *know*,' I said.

'Fudge,' Mom said, 'come out from under the table right now. Otherwise we won't have time for a story.'

'I want Grandma to read tonight.'

'I'd be honoured,' she told him.

'Will you read me a story about the green stuff?'

'I'm not sure you have any books about the green stuff,' Grandma said. 'But maybe I can make up a story about a little boy who liked money so much—'

'So much, what?' Fudge asked. 'So much he ate it?'

'You'll find out when you're in bed and I tell you the *whole* story,' Grandma said. From the way she pressed her lips together, I could tell she was wondering how she was going to get out of this one.

The next morning Grandma reported that Fudge had been engrossed by her story about a boy who went to Washington to learn how money was made. Mom and Dad took that as an omen.

'A trip certainly couldn't hurt,' Mom said. 'Remember when you took me on that tour?' she asked Grandma.

'Yes, I do,' Grandma said.

'It might even help Fudge understand,' Dad agreed. 'Good idea, Muriel!'

Grandma beamed.

'We haven't been to Washington in ages,' Mom said.

'I've *never* been there,' I told them. 'Jimmy Fargo says the Air and Space Museum is so cool. Can we check it out?'

'Sounds good to me,' Dad said.

Grandma volunteered to stay at our apartment with Tootsie, Turtle and Uncle Feather. And a week later, when school was closed for two days because of teachers' meetings, we headed for Washington, D.C.

We started out early and ate breakfast on the train. Fudge was really impressed by the buffet car. As soon as we carried our food to our seats, he was ready to go back for more. Mom and Dad were sitting in the row in front of us, so I

was the one he kept annoying. 'Come on, Pete, let's go back to the buffet car.'

'I'm still eating,' I told him, slurping up the last of my juice.

He was quiet for about two minutes. Then he asked, 'Are we almost there, Pete?'

'No, we're not almost there. We're not even close. It takes three hours to get to Washington, so why don't you look at your books, or draw a picture or something.'

I got out my Electroman Advanced Plus. But just as I started a game Fudge covered the screen with his hand. 'Will you take me back to the buffet car now?'

'If I do, will you leave me alone?'

'Sure, Pete.'

I asked Dad for money. He reminded me not to get Fudge any candy, as if I needed reminding. He was already flying high. 'A banana would be good,' Dad said. 'And juice, not soda.'

The buffet car was three cars forward. Fudge had already learned to open the doors between the cars by kicking the *open door* plate at the bottom of each door. He liked the whoosh of air as he raced from car to car. 'This is so fun, Pete! I wish we could ride the train every day.'

'We ride the subway,' I reminded him.

'But there's no buffet car on the subway and the seats aren't soft and when you look out the window it's all dark.'

'That's because the subway is an underground train.'

'Wow, Pete, I never knew that!'

'Well, now you know.'

'William says, *Learn something new every day*.' I snorted.

'William is smart, Pete. He's the smartest teacher in the world.'

Sure he is, I thought.

Fudge got a banana and a juice box at the

buffet car. While I paid, Fudge peeled all the skin off his banana and shoved half of it into his mouth. His cheeks puffed out and he couldn't talk his mouth was so full. He insisted on carrying the little cardboard box that held the rest of his banana and his juice box. But on the way back from the buffet car the train swerved and Fudge lost his balance. He flew into the lap of a woman in a red suit and coughed out the gooey, half-chewed banana all over her clothes.

'Get off me!' she shouted. 'Someone get him off me!' She shoved Fudge off her lap as if he were a slobbering dog, or worse. 'Ohhhh,' she cried, 'look what you've done. You've ruined my suit.' She turned to the man across the aisle. 'Can you believe this? And I've got an appointment at the White House!' Then she glared at Fudge, who was picking himself up off the floor. 'You know who lives at the White House?' she asked him.

'The President,' Fudge said.

'That's right! And I'm going to tell him exactly how I got these stains on my suit.' She jumped up and marched to the rear of the car, where there was a rest room.

'Tell him it was a banana,' Fudge called. 'And tell him my name, too. It's Farley Drexel Hatcher, but he can call me Fudge.'

I grabbed him and pulled him back to our seats. No way was I ever taking him to the buffet car again.

When we finally got to Washington our first stop was a tour of the Bureau of Printing and Engraving. That's where the green stuff is printed. There were about twenty other people in our group. Our tour guide's name was Rosie. She had dark eyes, reddish hair and big teeth.

Before our official tour began, Rosie told us some of what we'd see during our tour. *Fun Facts*, she called them. I decided to write her

Fun Facts in my notebook in case any of my teachers ever assigned a report on US currency.

'Fun Fact Number One,' Rosie said. 'The Bureau of Printing and Engraving produces thirty-seven million notes a day, worth about $696 million.'

Fudge raised his hand and asked, 'Are notes the same as bucks?'

Rosie told him they were. 'They're called bills, dollars, bucks—'

Some guy shouted out, 'How about moola?' A couple of people laughed. A few more groaned.

'Well, yes,' Rosie said. 'I suppose some people refer to money as moola or even as dough.'

'How about green stuff?' Fudge shouted. 'That's what my grandma calls it.'

This time almost everyone in our group laughed. Any minute I thought Fudge would take a bow. But Rosie kept checking her watch and asked the group to hold their questions and

comments until she was finished running through all her Fun Facts. Then she led us through the metal detector. Fudge asked if we were getting on a plane. Rosie explained that we weren't, but because this is a federal building they had to make sure no one was carrying a weapon.

'A weapon?' Fudge said, right before Dad set off the alarm. Nobody would have paid any attention except that Fudge shouted, 'Dad! Are you carrying a weapon?' That got everyone's attention.

'It's his belt buckle, Turkey Brain,' I said.

Rosie took a deep breath and checked her watch a couple of times. She was still smiling but she didn't look that happy. She led us down a long hallway. We followed her single file through narrow corridors that twisted and turned. The old wooden floor squeaked under us. Every few minutes we'd stop in front of glass walls that looked down into rooms where we could see the

green stuff in production. As the crowd pressed forward to the window wall, Fudge worked his way up front, wedging himself between people's legs if he had to, to get a better view. Then he waved to the workers in the rooms below. I heard him singing under his breath, *'Oh, money, money, money, I love money, money, money . . .'*

I couldn't believe my parents thought bringing him here was a good idea.

We saw the green stuff as it was printed, cut, stacked and counted. Towards the end of the tour Rosie invited Fudge to walk with her since he was so interested. 'I love money!' he told her.

'Well, you've come to the right place,' Rosie said.

'Want to see mine?' He pulled out a jumble of Fudge Bucks. 'I make it myself. Pretty good, huh?'

'Play money is fine,' Rosie told him, 'as long as you don't try to use it or pass it off as real because then you could get in big trouble.'

'Why?' Fudge said.

'Because that's the rule,' Rosie said, firmly, which shut him up until the end of the tour. That's when Rosie asked our group if anyone had any special questions. Fudge's hand shot up first. Rosie didn't look thrilled but she had no choice. She had to call on him.

'I still need to find out how you get a lot of it all at once,' Fudge said.

'A lot of . . .' Rosie sounded confused.

'Money!' Fudge shouted.

Mom stepped in and tried to explain. 'Fudge has become very curious about money,' she told Rosie. 'And we thought that by bringing him here . . .'

'I hear what you're saying,' Rosie said to Mom. 'But somebody has to set him straight.'

'I'll set him straight,' a tall man with silver hair said. 'First of all, young man, you need to get a good education. Then, when you're

grown up, you need a good job. Then you save something from your salary every week. You invest carefully. You let your money work for you. And by the time you're my age, with luck, you'll have a nice little nest egg for your retirement.'

Our group applauded.

But Fudge still wasn't satisfied. 'Or else someone can just give it to you,' he said.

You could hear the tongues clucking and the whispers in the crowd. I heard someone say, 'This kid is hopeless.'

That's when Rosie announced that the next tour was about to begin and we could all proceed to the gift shop. 'You're going to love the gift shop,' she told Fudge. 'All the children do.'

'Gift shop?' Mom said. 'Warren, did you know there was a gift shop?'

Dad groaned.

8
Cousin Coincidence

Rosie was right. Fudge loved the gift shop. Everything in sight had a money motif. *Everything.* Shirts, socks, ties; pencils, notepads, snow globes; you name it – it was done up as money.

'This is better than the tour!' Fudge sang, racing all around. He was fascinated by a five-pound bag of shredded money containing a minimum of ten thousand dollars. You could buy it for forty-five dollars. 'Pete, look, ten thousand dollars all in one little bag.'

'Yeah, but it's shredded, so it's totally useless.'

'I could try to glue it back together. Then we could buy every toy in the world.'

'Even if you could glue it back together, it'd be counterfeit,' I told him. 'If you tried

to use it, you'd go to prison.'

'Anyway,' Dad said, 'forty-five dollars is way too much to spend.'

'How about a five-dollar bag instead?' the clerk suggested, holding one up.

Fudge liked that idea. 'I'll get one for me and one for Richie.'

'Richie Richest doesn't need shredded money,' I told him.

'How about you, Pete?'

'I don't need it either. I don't even want it.'

'OK, fine,' Fudge said. 'Then I'll just get a bag for me.'

While Dad was paying, Fudge tore around the shop. 'How about this tie?' he shouted. 'I have to have this tie! Mom, please can I have this money tie?'

Mom hustled over to him. 'What are you going to do with a tie?'

'Wear it,' Fudge said. 'Please, Mom! Pretty,

pretty please with pistachio nuts on top.'

'All right.' Mom gave in. 'But that's it.'

'What about Tootsie?' Fudge said.

'Tootsie doesn't need anything from this shop,' Mom said. 'She doesn't understand about money.'

'*Yet*,' Fudge said. Then he took off again, laughing like a lunatic.

I turned to Mom and Dad. 'So, you think he's cured now?'

They looked at me like *I* was the lunatic. Then Dad said, 'Let's just get out of here.'

While we were collecting our things, Fudge raced back across the gift shop. 'Dad,' he said. 'That guy is staring you out.'

'What guy?' Dad asked.

'*That* one,' Fudge said, pointing across the shop.

'Don't point,' Mom told Fudge. 'It's not polite.'

101

'Then how will Dad know *which* guy I mean?'

'Good question,' I said. 'It's pretty crowded in here.'

'Peter, please . . .' Mom said, shaking her head. Then she turned to Fudge. 'You can describe him, instead of pointing.'

'OK,' Fudge said. 'That guy, who kind of looks like you, is staring you out, Dad.'

'It's not *staring you out*,' I told Fudge for the twentieth time, at least. 'It's *staring at you*.'

Now some guy came across the room and walked right up to Dad. He was big – taller and heavier than Dad. His voice boomed through the room, 'You have the Hatcher jaw and the Hatcher eyes and if I didn't know better I'd swear you must *be* a Hatcher!' He stuck out his hand and introduced himself. 'Howard Hatcher of Honolulu, Hawaii.'

For a minute Dad looked blank. Then he did a double take. 'No,' he said. 'It can't be. Are you

102

telling me you're Cousin Howie Hatcher?'

'None other. And you're Cousin Tubby, aren't you?'

'Cousin *Tubby*?' Fudge said.

I was thinking exactly the same thing but I don't always *say* what I'm thinking, the way Fudge does.

'I'm known as Warren now,' Dad told Cousin Howie.

Cousin Howie gave Dad a friendly punch in the shoulder. 'Lost a few pounds since we last met, huh? You were a real butterball in those days.' He laughed. 'A big old tub of lard.'

Dad sucked in his gut and stood up really straight.

'You got to work out, Tub!' Howie said, sticking his finger in Dad's gut, like Dad was the Pillsbury Doughboy.

'I do work out, Howie.' Dad got a funny look on his face then, like he suddenly wished he'd

told this guy he must be mistaken. Like he had no long-lost cousin named Howie.

'Well, maybe you got to work harder,' Cousin Howie said. 'Run a marathon or two.' That struck me as weird, because Dad was a lot less flabby looking than Cousin Howie, who had shifted his focus to Fudge and me. I stood up straight, shoulders back, stomach tight.

'See, that's why we used to call him *Tubby*,' Cousin Howie said, as if we didn't get it by now. 'So, Tub, these handsome boys belong to you?'

Dad said, 'Yes, this is my family. My wife, Anne . . .'

Cousin Howie kissed Mom's hand. 'So you're the little lady who stole Tubby's heart.' Mom looked like she might puke.

'And these are my sons,' Dad said. 'Peter and Fudge.'

'Fudge!' Cousin Howie said. 'Now there's a name.'

'Actually, it's Farley Drexel,' Dad said. 'We just call him Fudge.'

'Farley Drexel!' Cousin Howie's voice was so loud I backed away. 'What a coincidence.'

Fudge pulled me aside. 'What's a coincidence?' he asked.

'It's like when something just happens, something you didn't expect.'

'We didn't expect Cousin Howie, did we?'

'No,' I told him. 'We definitely didn't expect Cousin Howie. But he's more of a surprise than a coincidence.'

Cousin Howie wasn't alone. He introduced us to his wife, Eudora, a chunky woman with freckles, a doll's mouth and straw-coloured hair. 'Sweetheart,' he said, 'I want you to meet my long-lost cousin, Tubby Hatcher.'

'Warren,' Dad said, with a tight smile on his face.

'Right you are,' Cousin Howie said. 'You keep

reminding me and eventually I'll remember.'

Dad took a deep breath while Eudora gushed. 'I have heard so much about you over the years, Tubby.'

'Warren,' Dad said again. 'My name is *Warren.*'

'Oh, of course,' she said, laughing. 'You wouldn't go by your boyhood nickname any more, would you? I mean, imagine a grown man called *Tubby.* That would be embarrassing, wouldn't it?'

'Actually,' Dad told her, ' Howie is the *only* person who ever called me Tubby.'

'Is that right?' Howie said. 'And I always thought *everybody* called you Tubby.'

Eudora smiled sweetly and turned to Dad. 'What a shame you lost touch when Howie's family moved to Hawaii. I know how much Howie's missed you.' After that she took Mom's hand and said, 'I feel as if we're

106

personally connected, don't you?'

Before Mom had a chance to answer, before she could say, *Why no, I don't feel personally connected at all. Why would anyone in her right mind feel personally connected to you and Cousin Howie?* Eudora gushed, 'This is just so wonderful. We didn't think we had any family left. And to find you this way, out of the blue . . .' She pulled Mom close and hugged her until Mom was practically gasping for breath.

Mom looked to Dad for guidance when suddenly Fudge said, 'It's a real coincidence.'

Eudora looked surprised. 'Why, yes . . . it is. A real coincidence.'

I thought it was a pretty weird coincidence since Dad's never mentioned anything about a Cousin Howie to us.

And there were still more family members to meet. Eudora whistled and two girls about my age came over. 'Boys,' she said to Fudge and

me, 'meet your long-lost cousins, Flora and Fauna Hatcher. They're named for the natural beauty of our islands. And that's just what we call them . . . our natural beauties.'

Fudge laughed. It came out sounding like a big hiccup. I gave him an elbow and he covered his mouth with his hand. Isn't he the one who told me we don't laugh at people's names? Not that I didn't feel like laughing about Flora and Fauna too. But I was into proving I could control myself. It was part of my new seventh-grade maturity.

Eudora went back to talking with Mom and Dad, leaving Fudge and me with the Natural Beauties.

'We're twins,' one of them said.

'Identical, in case you didn't notice,' the other one added.

'You want to know how to tell us apart?' the first one asked.

'By your fingerprints?' Fudge asked.

'In case you don't have access to our fingerprints,' the second one said, 'I'm Flora and I have a scar on my chin.' She stuck out her chin and pointed underneath to her scar. 'See?'

Then the other one said, 'I'm Fauna and I have a brown dot in my right eye, but you have to look really close to see it.'

Who'd want to? I was thinking as Fudge stood on tiptoe and peered into Fauna's right eye.

'How old are you?' Flora asked me.

'He's twelve,' Fauna said, stretching back to her full height, which was just a little taller than me.

'How'd you know that?' I asked her.

'I can always tell,' Fauna said.

'How old are you?' I asked.

'How old do you think?' Fauna said.

'I'm not into guessing,' I told them.

'He's not into guessing,' Fauna repeated

to Flora and they giggled.

Why do girls giggle? I mean, do they really find things so hysterically funny, or are they born that way?

'Want to know how old *I* am?' Fudge asked. He didn't wait for them to answer. 'I'm five but I'll be six soon. I'm in mixed group.'

'What's mixed group?' Flora asked.

'It's what comes after kindergarten if you're really smart,' Fudge told her. 'Pete's in seventh grade.'

'That's what grade we'd be in—' Flora said.

'If we went to school,' Fauna said, finishing for her.

'You don't go to school?' Fudge asked.

'We're home schooled,' Fauna said.

'What's that?'

'Our parents teach us at home,' Flora explained.

'Who else is in your class?' Fudge asked.

'No one,' they answered together.

'Except our brother sometimes hangs around,' Flora said. That's when I realized the little boy hiding behind her was part of the family.

'He's almost four,' Fauna said, 'and even though you can't tell—'

'Our mother is pregnant again,' Flora whispered.

'Our mother was pregnant one time,' Fudge said, also whispering.

'Only one time?' Flora asked. She and Fauna looked at each other and giggled again.

'Isn't that right, Pete?'

'How about three times?' I said. 'Once with me, once with you, and once with our little sister.'

'Oh. I forgot about the you and me part,' Fudge said. Then he danced around, singing, 'I know how the baby got inside—'

'We all do,' I said, stopping him before he got started.

This time Flora and Fauna actually laughed. Then Flora stepped aside and said, 'This is our little brother. And if you think we have interesting names, wait till you hear his!'

'It's Farley Drexel!' Fauna announced.

'*Farley Drexel?*' Fudge said. 'That's *my* name!'

'It can't be,' Flora told him.

'Well, it is,' Fudge said, hands on his hips.

'But it's an old family name,' Fauna said.

'Yeah, well, our fathers are cousins, remember?' I said.

'You mean—' Flora began.

'That Farley Drexel Hatcher—' Fauna said.

'Was *your* father's uncle just like he was *our* father's uncle?' Flora finished for both of them.

I nodded. 'We call him Fudge,' I said.

'They call me Fudge,' Fudge repeated. 'Everybody but my little sister calls me Fudge.

She calls me Foo, but that's just because she can't say Fudge.'

'Fudge! That's a great name,' Fauna said. 'We've been trying to come up with—'

'A good name for Farley,' Flora said.

'And Fudge is perfect!' Fauna added.

'He can't have my name,' Fudge told them.

'He already does,' I reminded him.

'He has the Farley Drexel part but not the *Fudge*!' Fudge planted his feet wide apart and prepared to do battle. 'You can call him Farley or you can call him Drexel or you can call him F. D., but you *can't* call him Fudge!'

That sounded familiar. I was wondering where I'd heard it before when Fudge nudged me and said, 'Remember when Rat Face said that, Pete?'

Oh yeah . . . I thought. *Rat Face. His first kindergarten teacher.* Then I started to laugh.

Little Farley growled.

'My name belongs to me,' Fudge told them, in case there was any doubt. 'I own it!'

'You can't own a name,' Flora said.

'Can too!' Fudge insisted.

Little Farley growled again. Fudge looked at him. 'Can't he talk?'

'Of course he can talk,' Flora said.

'But he doesn't have to because—' Fauna said.

'We say everything for him.' Flora finished the sentence. Having a conversation with the Natural Beauties was like watching two guys playing a video game. You got dizzy from trying to follow it.

When Little Farley growled a third time, Fauna said, 'He likes to pretend he's a bear.'

'Or a lion,' Flora added.

'I don't care if he's a bear *or* a lion,' Fudge told them. 'He can't have my name!'

This time, Little Farley bared his teeth.

114

'I think we should call him Fudge-let,' Fauna said to her sister.

'Or Fudge-kin,' Flora suggested.

'Oh, I like that,' Fauna said. She put her arm around her little brother.

'Why don't you just call him Mini,' I said.

'Minnie?' Flora said.

'As in *Mouse*?' Fauna asked.

'No,' I told them. 'As in Mini-Fudge.' In case they still didn't get it, I spelled it for them. 'M-i-n-i.'

'Mini-*Farley*,' Fudge shouted. 'Because there's only one Fudge and that's me!'

Mini-Farley got down on all fours, growled at Fudge, then attacked, grabbing Fudge's pants leg in his mouth. Fudge tried shaking him off but Mini held on, pulling and twisting until Fudge lost his balance and crashed to the floor. As he did, he let out a bloodcurdling scream. That got the attention not only of all four parents,

but everyone else in the gift shop.

'Stop that, Farley!' Flora shouted, as Fauna pulled him off Fudge.

Dad rushed to Fudge, kneeled beside him, and checked his leg.

'Dad,' Fudge cried, 'tell them they can't steal my name!'

'Nobody's *stealing* your name,' Dad said, trying to soothe him.

'Promise?' Fudge asked, wiping his nose with his sleeve.

'Actually,' Fauna said, 'we're just borrowing it.'

'No fair!' Fudge said. 'You have to ask if you want to borrow something. Right, Dad?'

'That's how it's usually done,' Dad agreed.

'Then let's just say we're . . .' Flora began, looking at her sister.

'Copying your name,' Fauna said.

116

'Copying?' Fudge asked.

'Yes,' Flora said. 'And copying is the highest form of flattery.'

'If you want to copy you have to pay two million dollars,' Fudge told them.

The Natural Beauties laughed. 'Your brother's hilarious,' Fauna told me.

'Don't you know the best things in life are free?' Flora asked Fudge.

As if that were some kind of cue, the Natural Beauties put their heads close together, hummed a note, and next thing I knew they started singing, right there in the middle of the gift shop.

The moon belongs to everyone
The best things in life are free,
The stars belong to everyone
They gleam there for you and me . . .

I backed away, hoping to disappear into the crowd that had gathered around them. *This is worse than Fudge's tantrum at the shoe store*, I thought. *I never should have come to Washington. I should have stayed in New York with Grandma. Or gone to Jimmy Fargo's. Anything but this. Absolutely anything!*

Finally, I was saved by the guard who came over and suggested that if we were finished shopping we might like to continue the show elsewhere. *Yes! Thank you, guard. Thank you for saving me.*

9
The Panda Poop Club

'Hot-fudge sundaes all around,' Cousin Howie barked at the waiter at the coffee shop. Then he added, 'Better make them doubles.'

I should have known the guard at the Bureau of Printing and Engraving couldn't save me. I should have known Dad and Cousin Howie would want to catch up and talk about old times. Not that Cousin Howie was happy when Mom and Dad both said they'd prefer no-fat frozen yogurt to ice-cream sundaes. You could see the disappointment on his face. He told the waiter to bring them a side order of hot fudge, just in case. 'In honour of Uncle Farley Drexel,' Cousin Howie said to Dad. 'Remember how he loved his hot fudge, Tubby?'

'No,' Dad said.

'Then your memory's not what it used to be,' Cousin Howie said. 'Uncle Farley had a hot-fudge sundae every day of his life. I'm sure the reason you call your boy *Fudge* is because of Uncle Farley Drexel's love for it.'

'I don't think so,' Dad said.

Eudora laughed. 'Well, Tubby, either way it's a treat to be here with you and your family. Howie's told me so many stories about the two of you. About how close you were as boys and how you were both going to be forest rangers when you grew up.'

Forest rangers? I thought. *That's news to me.* I tried to imagine Dad as a forest ranger but I couldn't. He's such a city kind of guy.

'Howie's a park ranger,' Eudora said. 'He's been at all the national parks in Hawaii. On January second he's starting his new job at Everglades National Park. Until then we'll be

travelling around the country.'

'Everglades,' Dad said. 'That sounds exciting, Howie.'

'Yes, it does,' Cousin Howie agreed. 'How about you, Tubby? What do you do?'

'*Warren* is in advertising,' Mom answered. 'We live in New York City.'

'Advertising?' Cousin Howie's face clouded over. *'Advertising!'*

'That's right,' Dad said, and I was glad he sounded proud of his job.

'But how can that be, Tub?' Cousin Howie asked. 'Are you saying you broke your vows?'

'Howie,' Dad said, 'we were boys. Boys often change their minds when they become men.'

'Well, I am certainly disappointed to hear that,' Cousin Howie said, digging into his sundae. 'I never expected you to sell out.'

'What did you sell, Dad?' Fudge asked. 'How much did you get for it?'

121

'It wasn't a question of selling out, Howie,' Dad said, ignoring Fudge. 'It was a question of growing up and following my interests.'

You tell him, Dad! I thought. Then I got this picture in my mind of Jimmy and me meeting about twenty years from now. Jimmy's wife will remind me that he and I vowed to become professional sock hockey players. And I'll be – I don't know – a web designer or a movie director and Jimmy will get all worked up about it because he'll be star of the Vermont Blue Socks, the national sock hockey champions, and he'll tell me I sold out.

'This is saaaad news, Tubby,' Cousin Howie said, stretching out the word. 'Advertising doesn't help make the world a better place.'

'Oh yes,' Fudge said. 'I learn a lot from commercials.'

A lot of nothing, I thought.

122

'Commercials?' Cousin Howie said. 'You write commercials?'

Fudge licked his spoon and said, 'My dad invented the Juicy-O commercial, and the Toddle-Bike commercial, and the one for X-Plode cereal.'

The Natural Beauties gave Fudge a blank look.

'You know,' Fudge told them, 'from TV.'

'We don't have TV,' Fauna said.

'Pete,' Fudge said, 'did you hear that? They don't have TV.'

'And they aren't missing anything either,' Cousin Howie said.

Dad didn't respond. He was trying to be diplomatic, I could tell. But Fudge was like a train that couldn't be stopped. 'And last year my dad wrote a book,' he announced.

Now Cousin Howie relaxed his brow. 'A book! Well, that's more like it,' he said.

'Isn't that more like it, girls?'

'Yes, Daddy,' the Natural Beauties chanted. 'That's more like it!'

'What kind of book, Tub?' Cousin Howie asked.

But did Dad have a chance to answer? No! Turkey Brain wouldn't shut up. 'Longer than a Dr Seuss book,' he said, 'but shorter than an encyclopedia. Right, Dad?'

Dad tried to smile. He and Mom exchanged a look. Then Dad said, 'Actually, Howie, I was researching the history of advertising.'

Howie's face clouded over again. I noticed that when he scrunched up his forehead, his eyebrows crept together as if they were living things. 'History is one thing, Tub, but the history of advertising is a . . . is a . . .'

Eudora put her hand on Cousin Howie's arm. 'Now, Howie, let's remember it takes all kinds to make the world go round.'

124

The Natural Beauties jumped up, put their heads close together, and hummed a note.

Oh no! I thought. *They're going to do it again. Get me out of here!*

This time it was some song about how love makes the world go round. Not only did they sing, they danced. All around the coffee shop. Fortunately, only three other tables were occupied.

Fudge leaned close and whispered, 'Is this a show, Pete?'

Yeah, a freak show, I thought. But instead of answering Fudge's question I moaned and buried my head in my hands, grateful we weren't in New York, where I might have known someone, someone from school who would say, *Saw you having ice cream with those weird sisters. Hope you're not related.*

During the show, Mini buried his face in his ice-cream bowl and lapped up what was left of

his ice-cream sundae. Cousin Howie and Eudora didn't notice, not even when Mini reached for the side order of hot fudge and lapped that up, too. He reminded me of Turtle. That's exactly what he does when you give him leftover scrambled eggs.

When the Natural Beauties finished their act, everyone in the coffee shop applauded, even our waiter. Eudora beamed. 'They've been performing since they were six,' she told us. 'They're known across the Hawaiian Islands as the *Heavenly Hatchers.*'

This was even more embarrassing than I'd thought!

When the waiter brought the bill, Dad grabbed it. 'My treat,' he said.

Cousin Howie didn't argue. Neither did Eudora, who said, 'Thank you, Tubby. That was mighty fine ice cream. This is a day we'll always remember.'

126

I was thinking, *Oh yeah, we'll definitely remember today!* Then I pushed back my chair and stood up. 'So, Dad, we better get going.' I tapped my watch. 'Remember . . . the Air and Space Museum?'

'Air and Space Museum?' Fudge said. 'Do they have a gift shop?'

That night Mom called Grandma from our hotel, to find out how she was doing with Tootsie. The second she hung up, the phone rang. It was Cousin Howie. When Dad got off the line he said, 'Well, boys, Cousin Howie's invited you on a VIP tour of the National Zoo tomorrow morning.'

'Zoo?' Fudge asked. He was playing with the aeroplane he got at the Air and Space Museum.

'Yes,' Dad told him. 'And you know what they have at the National Zoo?'

'Tigers?' Fudge guessed, getting ready to launch his plane.

'I'm sure they do,' Dad said.

'How about elephants?' Fudge asked, pulling back the rubber band.

'Probably,' Dad said. 'And they also have pandas.'

'Pandas, like in the Imax movie?' Fudge let go of the plane, which came flying across the room right at me. I held up my new book – *A History of Aerial Warfare* – to protect my face and the plane crashed to the floor.

'Pete, look what you did to my plane!'

'That's nothing compared to what your plane would have done to my face.'

'OK, boys,' Mom said. 'How about getting into bed? Dad and I are pooped. And tomorrow's another busy day.'

I fell asleep and dreamed that the woman in the red suit, the one Fudge spat banana on,

128

was my math teacher. She asked me to show her how I solved my problem. I kept trying but I couldn't get the right answer. Then I was in a small plane. It was so dark I couldn't see the pilot's face. I had no idea who he was until he said, 'So, Pete . . .' That's when I jumped, even though I had no parachute. As I fell I passed the Natural Beauties, who were slowly floating down. 'Catch him,' Flora said. 'What for?' Fauna asked. Then I woke up. My heart was racing. I checked my watch. It had only been twenty minutes since Mom turned out the lights.

At eight the next morning, Dad delivered Fudge and me to Cousin Howie who was dressed in his park ranger uniform, sitting in the driver's seat of an official golf cart at the entrance to the zoo. 'You see, Tub, if you were a ranger you could get special privileges, too.' Eudora sat next to him, with Mini in her lap. The Natural Beauties sat in back.

'Hop aboard, boys,' Howie called. 'Really sorry we can't invite you to join us, Tub. But we're at the limit now.'

Dad didn't look at all sorry he couldn't go with us. 'Keep an eye on Fudge, Peter,' he called as he dashed off. I wanted to run after him. Going to an art museum with him and Mom had to be better than this. But before I had the chance, Howie floored it. 'Hang on, everybody!' he sang as he nearly mowed down a group of early morning joggers. Fudge grabbed hold of me as we zoomed along the road through the zoo. At one sharp curve the golf cart almost toppled. Mini laughed like crazy. The Natural Beauties shrieked and the one next to me – I think it was Flora – grabbed my arm and dug her fingernails into my flesh. On the next curve she practically ended up in my lap.

She cried, 'Daddy, slow down!'

But Cousin Howie yelled, 'Yip-eeee!' as he swerved and curved and drove like a total maniac.

'Yip-eee!' Mini yelled with him.

Finally, Eudora shouted, 'Howie, think of the example you're setting for our children!'

Cousin Howie slammed on the brakes. The rest of us fell forwards. 'Got carried away there for a minute,' Cousin Howie said. 'What do we do when we get carried away?'

'We stop and count to ten,' the Natural Beauties said, sounding relieved.

'And if that doesn't work?' Cousin Howie asked.

'We count to ten again,' the girls said.

'And that's exactly what I'm going to do,' Cousin Howie said. 'Let's all count together.' He took a deep breath, then counted to ten. The Natural Beauties counted along with him.

'I don't hear *everybody* counting,' Cousin Howie said, turning to look at me and Fudge. This time we counted along with the others. When we got to ten, Mini kicked his feet and shouted, 'Yip-eee!' again.

'Good . . . very good,' Cousin Howie said.

Later, when we met up with Mom and Dad, Fudge said, 'Look what Cousin Eudora got for me at the panda gift shop.' He held out a tiny stuffed panda. I'd bought the same one for Tootsie.

'How thoughtful of Eudora to buy you a souvenir,' Mom said.

'It's not the one I wanted,' Fudge said.

'The one he wanted cost four hundred and seventy-five dollars,' I told Mom and Dad. 'It was lifesize.'

'Fudge is such a scream,' Flora said.

'We've never met anybody like him,' Fauna said.

132

Who has? I thought.

'And look at this,' Fudge said, waving a certificate in Mom's face. 'I'm an official member of the Panda Poop Club.'

'The Panda Poop Club?' Mom said.

'Yes. I'm the only one who sniffed the poop and held it in my hands.'

'It was on a paper towel,' I reminded him.

'Even so, Pete.'

It's true he was the only one of us to hold it. We all sniffed it. But that was before we knew what it was. We thought it was a peeled sweet potato. It was the same colour as a sweet potato. It was shaped like one, too. So how were we supposed to know it was poop? It smelt like grass to me. That was before I found out grass and bamboo smell a lot alike.

Jane, the panda keeper, had signed Fudge's official certificate. 'When I get enough money I'm going to buy my own panda,' he'd told her.

'Where will you keep him?' Jane had asked.

'In my apartment. I'll have a very big apartment with a panda room. And when it's nice outside, I'll walk my panda in Central Park. Mom will cook him sweet potatoes and I'll have another room filled with bamboo. And I'll take his poop to school for sharing and let all the kids sniff it, especially Richie Potter.'

Now Fudge began to tell Mom and Dad everything he'd learned about pandas. 'Even though they look soft and cuddly, they're still wild animals. They have claws and sharp teeth. You know why their heads are so big? Because pandas are born to chew. Their jaws are so strong they can crunch bamboo. And they use their hands like raccoons do.'

'It sounds as if you learned a lot this morning,' Dad said.

'I did. Jane said I was a very good listener.

And guess what else? We got to feed carrots to the pandas. Everyone but Mini. He ate the carrot himself.'

Cousin Howie offered to drive us to the train station in his van. On the way we passed the White House. If Dad or Mom were president, I thought, this is where we'd live. I'd ask Jimmy to come down to hang out. We'd bowl and swim and have sock slides down the longest hallways. Then we'd see movies in the screening room and the family chef would make us popcorn. I'd give just one interview a week, maybe two, on MTV or Nickelodeon. I'd have an opinion on everything, especially books, video games, music, the Internet, and movies. *When Peter Hatcher speaks, young America listens!* That's what they'd say about me.

I was enjoying my fantasy until Fudge leaned close and whispered, 'I wonder what the President said?'

'About what?'

'About the banana on that lady's suit.'

'Probably he didn't even notice. And if he did, he'd be too polite to mention it.'

'You know what, Pete?' Fudge said, looking out the window of the van. 'Someday this will all be mine.'

'What will all be yours?'

'This place,' he said, as we passed the Lincoln Memorial and the Washington Monument. 'It'll be called Fudgington then.'

'Don't hold your breath,' I told him.

'I never hold my breath, Pete. Unless I'm underwater.'

When we got to the train station Dad asked Cousin Howie where they were heading next.

'New England, Tub,' Cousin Howie said, pulling into a passenger drop-off area.

I noticed Dad had stopped trying to get

them to use his real name.

'And a few weeks from now,' Cousin Howie continued, as we got our stuff out of the van, 'we'll be showing our little tribe the sights and sounds of your city.'

I dropped my suitcase. *Our city?*

'Only problem,' Howie said, 'is that we haven't been able to find a place to stay.'

'Maybe I can help,' Dad said.

'Why thanks, Tubby. We'd love to spend a few days in New York with you and your family.'

'What I meant,' Dad said quickly, 'is that maybe I can help you find a hotel.'

'A hotel?' Howie asked. 'Now why would we prefer a hotel to staying with you?'

'Our apartment is small,' Mom said. 'The boys share a divided room and Tootsie's crib is in a remodelled closet.'

'Not a problem for us,' Cousin Howie said. 'We have our camping gear right here, in the

van. Never travel without it. The Honolulu Hatchers are ready for whatever comes their way.'

'Yes, but, you see—' Mom began.

Eudora covered Mom's hand with her own. 'We're family, Anne. Wait till you see how little space we take up. We're used to making ourselves practically invisible, aren't we?'

Mini-Farley growled.

Eudora said, 'He's showing you how well he fits into the forest.'

West Sixty-eighth Street isn't exactly the forest, I thought.

'Up with the sun,' Cousin Howie said, 'and asleep with the moon. You'll hardly know we're there.'

Mom had this weak smile on her face as she looked at Dad.

Just say no! I begged, inside my head.

'Well, Howie,' Dad said, 'you'd be more than

welcome at our place. Just let us know when.'

'And give us some warning,' I said. *So I can arrange to stay at Jimmy's*, I was thinking.

'What Peter means,' Dad said, 'is give us some warning so he can clean up his room. Isn't that right, Peter?' Dad looked at me and I got the message.

'Yeah,' I said. 'Sure. That's exactly what I mean.'

10
Bird on Strike

When we got home Grandma told us Uncle Feather hadn't said a word since we left. 'I'm worried,' Grandma said. 'He could have a sore throat.'

'Uncle Feather's fine,' Fudge told her. 'He'll talk tonight.'

'How do you know?' I asked.

'I know my bird, Pete.' Fudge pulled a chair over to the kitchen counter, stood on it, climbed up, opened the cupboard, and pulled out a package of rice cakes.

'Don't spoil your appetite,' Grandma said. 'I've made you a nice supper.'

'Couscous and Moroccan chicken?' Not that I had to ask. Just catching whiffs from the oven

was enough to make my mouth water.

Grandma nodded. 'And Buzzy's coming up to join us.'

'Great,' I said. Grandma and Buzzy Senior met over the summer, in Maine. And as Mom likes to say, *one thing led to another*. They were married at the end of August. I really like Buzzy Senior. The only problem – and it's a big one – is he's Sheila Tubman's grandfather. The idea that I could be Sheila Tubman's step-something is revolting.

'Sheila's coming, too,' Grandma said.

I groaned.

'Now, Peter—' Grandma began.

I didn't wait for her to finish. 'Come on, Grandma, you knew about Sheila and me before you married Buzzy.'

'That doesn't mean you two can't be civil to one another.'

'What's *civil*?' Fudge asked, climbing on to

141

Grandma's lap with his rice cake.

Grandma stroked his hair. 'It means not being rude,' she told him, looking right at me.

'Fine,' I said. 'I'll be *civil*.'

'It could even mean being pleasant and respectful,' Grandma added.

'I'm pleasant and respectful,' Fudge said, munching away. 'Right?'

'Oh yeah,' I told him. 'You're the most pleasant and respectful person ever.'

He laughed and when he did, half of the chewed-up rice cake inside his mouth wound up on the floor. Turtle lapped it up like it was the world's best treat.

Grandma suggested Fudge try to keep his food in his mouth but Fudge told her, 'Turtle loves chewed-up food. Look . . .' And he let another mouthful go.

'That's enough, Fudge,' Grandma said.

'Finish your rice cake, then tell me all about Washington.'

'You mean *Fudgington*?' he asked.

That's when I took off for my room. Turtle padded down the hall after me. I stopped to have a look at Uncle Feather. 'How's it going?' I asked, standing right in front of his cage. He looked at me but he didn't say anything. So I said, 'Bonjour, stupid.' That's one of his favourite expressions. Once you get him started on that one, forget it. You can't turn him off. But this time, instead of repeating it over and over, he scratched his head with his foot.

'What's your problem?' I asked. 'Did you miss us? Is that it? Were you lonely?'

He picked up a rattle with his foot and shook it. He loves Tootsie's baby toys. But he still didn't say anything. So I tried some of his favourite words, the really bad ones, the ones Mom calls

143

thoroughly inappropriate. Turtle sat up, waiting. But Uncle Feather just yawned, like he was bored or tired. Either way, he had nothing to say.

Hmmm, I thought. *Maybe he does have a sore throat. Maybe he has laryngitis.*

Half an hour later, when Sheila came in with Buzzy Senior, she said, 'Did Muriel tell you about your bird, Fudge?'

'What about my bird?'

'He hasn't said a word since you left. I was up here yesterday and again this morning and he wouldn't speak at all.'

'He'll talk tonight,' Fudge said.

'I'd like to know how you can be so sure about that,' I said.

'I know my bird, Pete!' he said for the second time.

'I hope you're right,' Sheila said. Then she asked, 'So how was Washington?'

144

'You mean *Fudgington*?' Fudge said.

Sheila shook her head in disgust. 'Muriel,' she said, 'you *have* to do something about your youngest grandson. He thinks the world revolves around him.'

'The world revolves around the sun,' Fudge said. 'I learned that at the planetarium.'

Sheila just shook her head again.

That night, while I was on my bed, reading, I heard Fudge talking to Uncle Feather. 'Good night . . . sleep tight . . . don't let the monsters bite.'

And Uncle Feather answering, 'Good night, sleep tight . . . bite . . . bite . . . bite . . .'

I went into Fudge's room to see Uncle Feather for myself but Fudge had already covered his cage. 'Shush, Pete,' Fudge said. 'He's sleeping now.' Fudge was snuggled up with his bag of shredded money.

The next day it was the same thing. Uncle Feather wouldn't talk to any of us. But Fudge said, 'Don't worry. He'll talk tonight.'

Just as Fudge promised, that night I heard him talking to his bird. 'Everybody's worried about you, Uncle Feather. But you're fine, aren't you? You're a fine birdy.'

'Fine birdy . . . just fine . . . birdy, birdy.'

Fudge laughed.

The next day when Uncle Feather *still* wouldn't talk to me or Mom or Dad, I asked Fudge, 'How come he only talks to you?'

'Because I'm his favourite.'

'OK, let's say that's true. That still doesn't explain why he'll only talk at night.'

'Who can explain it, who can tell you why?' Fudge sang. That's a line from a song Buzzy sings to Grandma.

'Try,' I told him.

'Try what, Pete?'

146

'Try and explain why Uncle Feather only talks at night.'

'I can't, Pete.'

'How long has it been since he's only talked at night?'

'Since . . . since . . .'

I could tell he was stalling. 'I'm listening,' I told him.

'I know you are, Pete!'

'Well?'

'He only talks at night since Richie Potter was here for a play date.'

'What's Richie Potter got to do with it?'

Fudge shrugged.

'That's a pretty weird story, Fudge.'

'Weird stories happen, Pete.'

I shook my head. I didn't believe him for a minute. Not one minute. I know him too well. He was hiding something. So that night I waited outside his bedroom door. Since he's

147

afraid of monsters he never closes it all the way. He's got night lights plugged into every outlet in his room. And before he gets into bed he sprays the whole place with monster spray – which is nothing but scented water in a bottle with a fancy label. But he believes in it, so I've promised Mom and Dad I'll never tell.

This time, when Fudge said, 'Good night . . . sleep tight,' I crept into his room. I could see him on his bed, thumbing through one of his catalogues. 'Good night . . . sleep tight,' he said again. 'Don't let the monsters bite.'

'Good night . . . sleep tight,' came the reply. Only it wasn't coming from Uncle Feather. It was coming from my brother!

'Aha!' I called, jumping on to his bed. 'Gotcha!'

Fudge screamed. I guess I really scared him. Then he started bawling.

Dad came running into Fudge's room,

followed by Mom. She picked up Fudge. He clung to her. 'What's wrong, Fudgie . . . tell Mommy . . . where does it hurt?'

'You want to know what's wrong?' I said. 'I'll tell you.'

'No, Pete!' Fudge screamed through his tears. 'No!'

Mom and Dad looked puzzled. 'What's all this about?' Dad asked.

'I'll tell you what it's about,' I said, whipping the cover off Uncle Feather's cage. 'Uncle Feather's lost his voice and Fudge has been talking for him. I caught him in the act.'

'What?' Mom said.

'Your younger son is a good mimic,' I said. 'He almost got away with it.'

'How long has this been going on?' Dad asked. I half-expected Uncle Feather to answer, *It's been going on for weeks now. It's about time you noticed.*

149

'Peter . . .' Dad began.

'Don't ask me,' I said. 'Ask bird-boy.'

'Fudge?' Dad said.

Fudge buried his face in Mom's neck, slobbering all over her.

'How long has it been since Uncle Feather talked?' Dad asked.

'Since . . . since . . . since . . .' Fudge sobbed. 'Since Richie Potter's first play date.' His face was a mess of snot and saliva.

'But that was weeks ago,' Mom said.

'I . . . I . . . I . . . gave him my best marble . . . the green one and . . .'

'You gave Richie Potter your best marble?' Mom said. 'That was very generous of you.'

'No!' Fudge cried. 'I gave it to Uncle Feather. I put it in his cage and he swallowed it and now he can't talk.' That unleashed another round of sobbing.

'You fed Uncle Feather a marble?' I asked.

150

'I didn't feed him, Pete! I gave it to him to play with. I didn't know he was going to swallow it and stop talking.'

'Wait a minute,' I said. 'How could Uncle Feather swallow a marble? I mean, look at the size of him.'

We all looked over at Uncle Feather, who stared back at us.

'I gave it to him before I went to school and when Richie Potter came over the marble was gone and Uncle Feather wouldn't talk.'

'Was that the day Richie Potter wanted broccoli for his snack?' Mom asked.

'Does broccoli have something to do with Fudge's marble?' Dad said.

'I don't think so,' Mom said. 'Does it, Fudge?'

'No!' Fudge started crying again.

All this time Uncle Feather watched from his cage. If you ask me, he was enjoying the attention.

The next day Mom called the vet while Fudge danced around her. 'Don't forget to tell her about my marble,' he kept reminding Mom.

Finally, Mom said, 'My son wants to know if our bird could have swallowed his marble by accident.'

The vet must have said no because Mom shook her head and said, 'That's what we thought.' Then the vet must have asked Mom questions, because Mom said, 'His appetite is fine and he's drinking the same amount of water as usual.' After that it was, 'He loves his bath.' Then, 'Oh yes, he's his usual active self. He's just not talking. He won't say a word.' Then there were a couple of *uh-huh*s and three or four *I see*s from Mom. She reached for a notepad and wrote something down. 'Yes . . . well . . . thank you so much.' Then she hung up the phone.

Before Mom had the chance to tell us

152

anything, Fudge said, 'How does the vet know Uncle Feather didn't swallow my marble? Because if he didn't swallow it, where is it?'

'Probably with your missing shoe,' I told him.

'My shoe is on the subway, Pete!'

As if I didn't know.

Everybody had an idea. Sheila stood in front of Uncle Feather's cage and said, 'You need a bird therapist. Maybe something happened to him. Some kind of trauma. I read a book about a girl who stopped talking because something terrible happened to her.'

'Like what?' I said.

'I can't discuss it in mixed company,' Sheila said.

'Is that like mixed group?' Fudge asked.

'No,' Sheila told him.

'Anyway, nothing terrible happened to him,' I said.

'How can you be so sure, Peter?' Sheila asked.

'Because I live here, remember?'

'Maybe it happened while you weren't home,' Sheila said. 'You have to think like a detective.'

'Trust me, Sheila, I know what I'm talking about.'

'A truly trustworthy person never has to say *trust me!*' Sheila said. 'Isn't that right, Uncle Feather?'

Uncle Feather sneezed.

Richie Potter came over for a play date and offered Uncle Feather money to talk. 'Five dollars if you say my name.' He held up the five-dollar bill for Uncle Feather to see.

'You're bribing Fudge's bird?' I asked. 'What do you think Uncle Feather would do with five dollars?'

'I don't know,' Richie said.

'Well, think about it.'

'I guess he doesn't get to go shopping.' Richie

154

folded the bill until it was so small it practically disappeared. Then he stuck it back in his pocket.

'If you want to bribe him, try his favourite fruit,' I said. 'He loves pears.' Richie and Fudge dashed off to the kitchen.

Melissa said, 'My mom says her acupuncturist can fix anything.'

'Her what?' Fudge asked.

'Acupuncturist,' Melissa said. 'It's some kind of doctor. He sticks needles in you and you get better.'

'Nobody's sticking needles in Uncle Feather!' Fudge said.

Buzzy said, 'Tough love. That's the answer. Don't let him push you around, Fudge. Let him know who's boss.'

Grandma laughed and said, 'Really, Buzzy. Uncle Feather's not a teenager. He's a bird.'

Jimmy said, 'My parents got divorced because my father never talked to my mother.'

That's the first detail Jimmy's dropped about his parents' divorce.

'Uncle Feather's not married,' I reminded him.

'Maybe that's his problem,' Jimmy said. 'Maybe he wants a mate.'

I looked at Jimmy, waiting for more. But he just shrugged and said, 'It's a possibility.'

That night I studied *The Myna Bird Handbook*. I found out that if you have two mynas they don't relate to their humans in the same way. They relate to each other instead. So forget about another bird.

Fudge told everyone who would listen about Uncle Feather. In the elevator he told Mrs Chen, who's visiting her family from China. She speaks only three words in English – *OK* and *No problem*. But she listened to Fudge as if she understood exactly what he was saying. Then

she nodded and said, 'No problem.'

In the lobby he told Olivia Osterman. 'I once had a myna bird,' she said. 'My bird could say, *I love you, Livvie. I love you soooo much!*'

'Where's your bird now?' Fudge asked, speaking up, so Mrs Osterman could hear him.

'Oh, he's been dead for years,' Mrs Osterman said. 'Birds don't live as long as people. And most people don't live as long as me. I'm going to celebrate my ninetieth birthday soon. What do you think of that?'

'I think that makes you a lot older than me.'

'Good thinking,' Mrs Osterman told Fudge.

'I'm a very good thinker,' Fudge said.

'And sometimes I am, too,' she said, snapping her fingers. 'Because I just got an idea about your bird's problem. Maybe he's lost his hearing, like me.'

'But you can still talk,' Fudge said.

'Yes, but I wear hearing aids. If your bird

can't hear what you're saying, he might not talk back to you.'

I said, 'That's the first real idea anybody's had about why Uncle Feather's stopped talking.'

That night, after Tootsie went to sleep, we gathered in Fudge's room to find out if Mrs Osterman was right. While the rest of us sat on the bed, Dad tiptoed across the room and slammed Fudge's door. Uncle Feather heard it all right. He jumped off his perch, flapped his wings, and jerked his head from side to side. You could tell he was really upset.

So much for Mrs Osterman's idea.

The next day I went online and found a website called mynabird.com. I sent a message asking if anyone knew why a myna would stop talking. I got five messages back, but nobody could give me a definite answer.

Henry Bevelheimer came up to have a look. He watched Uncle Feather for half an hour. 'Uh-

huh,' he said. 'Just what I thought. Your bird's on strike, Fudge.'

'On strike?' Fudge asked.

'Yes,' Henry answered. 'He's holding out for something. Now, all we have to do is figure out what.'

'More pears?' Fudge asked.

Mom said, 'More pears means more poop.'

'Uh-oh,' Fudge said. 'We don't want more poop.'

'What else could it be?' Henry asked. 'What else is really important to him?'

'Free time?' Fudge guessed. 'He likes free time a lot.'

'Don't we all,' Henry said.

'He already gets two free times a week,' I told Henry.

'Maybe he wants more,' Henry suggested.

'I don't think we can handle more than two free periods a week,' Mom said. 'Not with what

we have to go through every time he's out of his cage.'

What Mom meant is, mynas are known as frequent poopers, especially after they eat. So, when Uncle Feather's out of his cage, all the furniture has to be covered. We put old newspapers on the floor. Then we pull down the window shades and drape the mirrors because birds are attracted to light.

'But, Mom,' Fudge said. 'Maybe that's it.'

'Maybe it's not,' she said, thanking Henry for his time and showing him to the door.

'Sorry about that, Mrs H,' Henry said as he was leaving.

'It's all right, Henry,' Mom said. 'It's just that Fudge wants his bird to talk so badly he's willing to believe anything.'

'It must be tough on the little guy.'

'Yes,' Mom said, 'I think it is.'

Mom called the avian vet, someone who

only treats birds. That night after dinner, Mom and Dad sat Fudge down in the living room. Mom said, 'Fudge, this is what we're going to do. We're going to be kind and gentle to Uncle Feather. Friendly, but not pushy.'

Dad said, 'We're going to move his cage to a new spot for a while to see if that makes a difference.'

'Not out of my room,' Fudge cried. 'I can't sleep without Uncle Feather.'

'We'll move him to another part of your room,' Dad said. 'Maybe closer to the window, so he has a better view.'

'And then we're going to wait,' Mom said.

'For how long?' Fudge asked.

'As long as it takes,' Mom answered. 'That's the avian vet's advice.'

'And then he'll talk again?' Fudge asked.

'We hope so, but there are no guarantees,' Mom told him.

'If we had a million trillion bucks we could find a vet who would know how to fix him.'

'This has nothing to do with money,' Dad said. 'Money can't fix everything.'

'How do you know? You don't have a million trillion bucks.'

'That's true,' Mom said, 'we don't. But no amount of money will make Uncle Feather talk again. We just have to be patient and hope for the best.'

'Poor Uncle Feather,' Fudge said and tears rolled down his cheeks. 'It's so sad. Isn't it sad, Pete?'

'He doesn't seem sad,' I said, trying to sound upbeat.

'That's right,' Dad said. 'He's as playful as ever.'

Fudge shook his head. 'He just doesn't want us to know, so he's pretending.'

'What a thoughtful bird,' Mom said.

Fudge nodded. 'He takes after me.'

11
Baby Feet (Again)

Jimmy reminded me about the opening of his father's one-man show. Last summer Tootsie walked barefoot across one of Frank Fargo's wet canvases, leaving a path of little footprints in the blue paint. We thought Mr Fargo would go crazy when he saw what happened. Instead, he got an idea. He had Tootsie walk barefoot over two dozen wet canvases. And now those paintings were going to be on display in an art gallery in SoHo.

'I like shows,' Fudge said, as we were getting ready to go downtown.

'I know,' Dad said, zipping Fudge's jacket.

'Will they have singing or puppets?'

'No,' Dad said. 'Just paintings.'

'A show with just paintings?' Fudge was

surprised. 'Did you hear that, Pete? A show with just paintings!'

'Yeah, I heard.'

Mom came into the living room then, carrying Tootsie, who was dressed in some black velvet outfit that made her look like a baby movie star.

'Where's the babysitter?' Fudge asked.

'We don't need a babysitter tonight,' Mom told him, setting Tootsie down on the sofa.

'You're leaving Tootsie home by herself?' Fudge was even more surprised.

Mom laughed. 'No, we're taking Tootsie to the show.' She was trying to get fancy shoes on Tootsie's feet but Tootsie squirmed and kicked, making it impossible. Mom finally gave up and stuffed the shoes into the diaper bag.

'You're taking Tootsie?' Fudge couldn't believe it.

'Of course we're taking Tootsie,' Dad said.

'And just look at our girl. She's mighty pretty tonight, isn't she?'

'She's too young for a show,' Fudge argued. 'She won't understand it.'

'Without Tootsie there wouldn't be a show,' Dad reminded him.

Tootsie held her arms out to me. 'Uppy, Pee.' She waited for me to pick her up. When I did, she pulled my hair.

'Hey!' I said, which only made her laugh and pull harder.

Fudge hung on to me, tugging at my jacket. 'I don't want Tootsie to come with us. I want it to be just you and me, Pete.'

'I know how you feel,' I told Fudge, remembering all those times I didn't want *him* to come along. 'But you'll get over it.'

A banner announcing Frank Fargo's show hung outside the art gallery in SoHo. It said BABY

FEET in big, bold letters, and under that, FRANK FARGO. Inside, huge colourful paintings hung on the walls. When the canvases were spread out on the ground last summer, I didn't realize how big they would look hanging on a wall. You had to study them carefully to see the background of baby feet, but they were there, in every painting. The paintings had names like *Baby Feet Blueberry* and *Baby Feet Strawberry*. There was one called *Baby Feet Storm* and another called *Baby Feet Earth*.

Fudge looked around. 'Where's the stage?' he asked. 'Where're the seats?'

Dad explained. 'It's not that kind of show. It's more like going to an art museum for a special event.'

'Where's the event?' Fudge asked.

'This *is* the event,' Dad told him.

'No fair!' Fudge cried.

'Uh . . . Dad,' I said, hoping to escape before

166

things took a turn for the worse, 'I'm going to find Jimmy Fargo.'

'Take me,' Fudge cried. 'Please, Pete. Take me with you!'

I hesitated for a second, then gave in and grabbed Fudge by the hand. But it was crowded in the gallery and I didn't see Jimmy anywhere.

'I could walk across paintings, too,' Fudge told me. 'I could do it better than Tootsie. Tootsie doesn't go to school. She's not even toilet trained.'

'But she can make animal sounds,' I said, trying to keep it light.

'Who cares about her dumb *quack quack*s . . . and her stupid *miaow*s?'

People began to form a circle around Mr Fargo, who'd put Tootsie on his shoulders. 'Here she is,' Mr Fargo announced. 'The star of my show. The one, the only . . . Tootsie Pie!'

Tootsie laughed and grabbed hold of Mr

Fargo's hair. She's probably his biggest fan. And I'm not talking about his paintings. What does Tootsie know about art? For some reason none of us understands, Tootsie likes Mr Fargo. And Tootsie's the only person I know who can get Mr Fargo to smile. Which he did now, as flashbulbs went off. 'She's my inspiration!' Mr Fargo told the crowd. The crowd applauded.

'Is Tootsie famous?' Fudge asked.

'Yeah, just for tonight,' I answered. 'And she probably won't even remember.'

'I was famous once . . . right, Pete?'

'Yeah, you were famous for about a week when you rode the Toddle-Bike for Dad's TV commercial.'

'I remember.' He looked up at me. 'How about you, Pete? Were you ever famous?'

'Not yet.'

'Don't feel bad. You're famous to me.' He gave me a big smile and squeezed my hand.

'Thanks, Fudge.'

When Dad caught up with us, I said, 'It would be cool to have a painting by Frank Fargo, especially one with Tootsie's footprints.'

Fudge broke away from us and reached out to touch *Baby Feet Strawberry*. 'How about this one?'

Dad grabbed him from behind and pulled him back. 'No touching,' he said.

'Why not?' Fudge asked.

'Because your hands might not be clean.'

'They're clean. Look,' he said, holding them up for Dad to see.

'Even so,' Dad said, 'you aren't allowed to touch paintings on display.'

'Why not?' Fudge asked.

'That's the rule,' Dad said.

'It's a stupid rule,' Fudge said.

'We don't say the *stupid* word,' Dad reminded him.

'Yes, we do,' Fudge said. 'We just don't say it

about people. If we want to say it about people, we say *Turkey Brain*. Ask Pete. He knows.' Now Fudge pointed to *Baby Feet Storm*. 'How about this one? This one would look good in my room.'

'We can't afford these paintings,' Dad said. 'Look at the prices.' He pointed to the numbers on the title cards.

'Those are prices?' I asked. There weren't any dollar signs. Just a number, followed by three zeros, making every painting six or seven or eight thousand dollars.

'More zeros means more money, right, Pete?'

'I'll say!'

'So that's good, right?'

'Depends on if you're the seller or the buyer,' I told him.

'Which are we?'

'Neither,' Dad said. 'We're friends.'

'No zeros for friends,' Fudge sang.

Dad asked me to keep an eye on Fudge while

he went to greet someone he knew.

'I can't believe this,' I said, more to myself than Fudge.

'What can't you believe, Pete?'

'That somebody's going to pay seven thousand dollars for this painting.'

'So, Pete . . .' he began, and he got this greedy look in his eyes. I knew what was coming before he even said it. But he said it anyway. 'We could get Tootsie to do the same thing at home and then—'

I interrupted. 'Yeah, except nobody would pay us thousands of dollars for a painting.'

'How come?'

'Because we're not artists like Mr Fargo.'

'But, Pete, that doesn't make any sense.'

'What can I say, Fudge? That's the way it is.'

He swung my arm up and down. 'We think the same way, don't we?'

Before I could answer, before I could say, *No,*

we don't think the same way and we never will, someone came up from behind and stuck a finger in my ribs. I spun around.

'Gotcha!' Jimmy laughed.

'Where've you been?' I asked. 'I've been looking everywhere for you.'

'Yeah, it's crowded in here. That's a good sign. So, what do you think?' He stepped away from the paintings and studied them from a distance. He squinted, then made his fists into binoculars and peered through them. I did the same, and when I did, all those swirling colours looked like they were moving.

'Cool, huh?' Jimmy said.

'Yeah, amazing.'

'You're not thinking you could do the same thing, I hope?'

'No. Why would I be thinking that?'

'I don't know. You just have that look on your face.'

'What look?'

'Never mind.'

A woman in a black dress and dangling earrings shaped like skyscrapers stuck a red dot on the *Baby Feet Storm* card. She looked familiar – tall and scrawny with a lot of curly hair and a really long neck.

'Yes!' Jimmy pulled a victory fist. 'There goes another one.'

'Another what?' I said.

'Another painting. When a red dot goes up, it means that painting is sold.'

'Wow!' I said. 'Seven thousand dollars. What's it like to know your dad is rich and famous?'

'Rich?' Fudge said.

Jimmy ignored him and eyed me. 'First of all, the gallery gets half of everything. Second of all, since when are you so *into* money?'

'Me, *into* money?' I said. 'That's a joke! You

want to see someone who's into money, look at my brother.'

Fudge started singing, '*Money, money, money, I love money, money, money* . . .' Then he skipped away.

A minute later someone tapped me on the shoulder. 'Well, well, well,' she said. 'If it isn't my old friend, Peter Hatcher.' It was the woman in the skyscraper earrings. She was carrying a shoulder bag with a small dog inside. As soon as I heard her voice I recognized her. It was Giraffe Neck, this woman I knew last year when we lived in Princeton. She owned a gallery there, right near the movie theatre. One of Frank Fargo's paintings hung in the window. It was called *Anita's Anger*. One time I went in and told Giraffe Neck I personally knew Frank Fargo. But what was she doing here? And why was she carrying a Yorkie in her bag? I reached out to pet the dog but it barked at me.

'It's OK, Vinny,' Jimmy said, scratching the dog behind his ears. 'Peter's a friend.'

'You know her dog?' I asked.

'Sure, I know Vinny,' Jimmy said. 'He walks backwards even when he's barking at you.'

'Backwards?'

'He retreats,' Giraffe Neck explained.

'Yeah, that's it,' Jimmy said. 'He retreats.'

'But he loves Jimmy,' Giraffe Neck said, tousling Jimmy's hair. 'Vinny never barks at Jimmy.' Then she was gone, back to doing business.

Jimmy watched her for a minute, then turned back to me. 'What?' he said, as if I'd asked a question, which I hadn't.

'I didn't say anything,' I told him.

'But you were going to.'

'Well yeah, now that you mention it, didn't you say something about getting a Yorkie?'

Jimmy nodded.

'I thought so.'

A few minutes later I caught a glimpse of Giraffe Neck across the room with Mr Fargo. It looked like he was nuzzling her neck. Jimmy saw me watching them.

'Am I missing something here,' I began, 'or are your father and Giraffe Neck . . .'

'They're going out,' Jimmy said. 'They're talking about getting married.'

'Married?'

'Could you not say it like that?

'Like what?'

'Like it's a disaster or something.'

'I didn't say it's a disaster,' I told him. 'I'm just surprised, that's all. I mean, I'm supposed to be your best friend, so how come you didn't say something about your father marrying Giraffe Neck until now?'

'It wasn't official,' Jimmy said. 'And her name's Beverly. Beverly Muldour. And if you want to know, she's pretty cool.'

'If you say so.'

'The only bad thing is this means my parents aren't getting back together.'

'Did you think they would?'

Jimmy didn't answer.

'Come on, Jimmy, your parents can't stand each other. That's why they're divorced.'

'I don't want to hear that,' Jimmy said. 'Especially from you. You just said you're supposed to be my best friend.'

'OK, I'm sorry.'

'Just because they're divorced doesn't mean I want either one of them to marry someone else.'

'But you said Giraffe Neck's cool.'

'Yeah, but what does she know about being a parent?'

'Look at it this way,' I said. 'Your father doesn't know much about being a parent either.'

'You can say that again.'

'So how bad could it be? Your father seems happy tonight.'

'That's tonight.'

'So, maybe he'll be happier more of the time.'

Jimmy shrugged. 'Beverly says she won't try to be my mother since I already have one. She says we'll be friends instead. But what does that mean?'

'I don't know. Maybe you should just wait and see.'

It was after 9.00 p.m. by the time we got home. Tootsie was asleep in Dad's arms. Henry met us at the door to our building. 'Mrs H . . .' he said, 'you've got visitors.'

'Visitors?' Mom asked. 'At this hour? Warren, are you expecting anyone?'

Dad said, 'I can't imagine who it could be.'

'I know!' Fudge said. 'It's Grandma and Buzzy.'

'No, it's not your grandma,' Henry said,

handing a note to Mom.

'Then I'll bet it's William, my teacher.'

'Why would your teacher come to your house at night?' I asked.

'Because he likes me,' Fudge answered.

'Not everything's about you,' I told him while Mom opened the note.

She read it aloud. *Dear Tubby* . . . she began.

Oh no! I thought.

'Oh goody,' Fudge sang. 'It's the Howies!'

'Let Mom finish reading,' I said.

Mom started again.

Dear Tubby and Anne,

We finally made it to the Big City.

We're in the van, parked right around the corner.

Can't wait to see you again.

Your loving cousins,

Howie, Eudora, Fauna, Flora and Farley

'Well,' Mom said. 'What a surprise.'

Surprise? I thought. *That's one way of putting it.*

Dad passed the sleeping Tootsie to Mom. 'You take her up and I'll go see about Cousin Howie.'

'I'll come, too,' Fudge said.

'It's way past your bedtime,' Mom told him. 'And tomorrow's a school day.'

'But I'm not tired,' Fudge said. 'Look . . . see how wide I can open my eyes?'

'All right, but don't be long,' Mom said. 'What about you, Peter?' she asked, as I followed her to the elevator.

'I'm feeling really tired,' I said. 'I think I should go right to bed.'

She tried to feel my forehead but with Tootsie in her arms it wasn't easy. 'You're not getting sick, are you?'

'Yeah, I am. But not the way you think.'

12

Camp Howie-Wowie

An hour later the Howies were sound asleep on our living-room floor. 'Up with the sun, asleep with the moon!' Cousin Howie had said. 'You'll hardly know we're here.'

I'll know, I thought.

And just like that they'd climbed into their sleeping bags and closed their eyes. Cousin Howie snored softly. Lined up next to him was Eudora, then Mini-Farley, followed by the Natural Beauties. They slept flat on their backs, like a row of hot dogs in their rolls. All that was missing was the mustard and the relish.

Turtle didn't get it. He kept sniffing them. He even tried licking Eudora's face, since no toes were available. But still, they didn't wake up.

Mom said I had to get Turtle into my room, and fast, but I couldn't lure him away from the Howies. 'Pssst,' I whispered, crawling around the living room on all fours, holding out a wedge of cheese. 'Come here, boy.' He didn't even look at me.

Mom motioned for me to come into the kitchen.

She was laying out plates, bowls and silverware.

'Would you count out nine juice glasses, Peter?'

'Are we having a midnight supper or what?'

'It's for tomorrow morning's breakfast,' Mom said.

I checked the cupboard. 'I hate to break it to you, Mom, but we don't have nine juice glasses. How about four?'

'I'll ask Dad to pick up some paper cups.'

'Where is Dad, anyway?'

'At the grocery store. We've got five extra mouths to feed in the morning.' When the phone rang Mom grabbed it on the first ring. 'I'll take it in the bedroom so I don't wake our guests.'

The second Mom left the kitchen, Fudge tore out of his room in his pyjamas and started jumping over the sleeping Howies, making Turtle bark. Still, they didn't stir.

'Maybe they're dead,' Fudge whispered to me.

'They're not dead.'

'How do you know?'

'Because they're breathing. Be quiet. You can hear them.'

Fudge listened. Then he said, 'It's better to breathe, right, Pete?'

'Yeah, it's definitely better to breathe.'

'Remember when I wanted to be a bird breather when I grow up?'

'That was a bird *breeder*,' I reminded him.

'Oh, right. A bird breeder.' He watched the Howies for a minute, then looked up at me. 'This is fun, isn't it, Pete?'

'No,' I told him. 'It's not fun.'

He followed me into the kitchen. 'How come?'

'How come?' I repeated. 'I'll give you five reasons how come.'

'But, Pete, Grandma says, *The more the merrier.*'

'Grandma's full of sayings. You don't have to believe all of them.'

'But I do.' He dragged a chair over to the counter, climbed up, opened the snack cupboard, and pulled out a pack of rice cakes. 'It's like a giant sleepover, isn't it?'

I could think of plenty of words besides *sleepover* to describe the situation but none that were appropriate to say in front of him.

When Mom came back to the kitchen and

found Fudge stuffing his face, she scooped him up and carried him back to his room, where he started singing:

The moon belongs to everyone
The best things in life cost money.
The stars belong to everyone
They're all so bright and funny.
Money money money
Funny funny funny
Bunny bunny bunny
Honey honey honey . . .

A minute later Turtle was howling. He loves to sing along with Fudge. I was glad Uncle Feather was still on strike. A trio would have been more than I could take tonight.

If I'd gone to bed then, I'd probably have been OK – annoyed, but OK. I mean, suppose *The Simpsons* were on tonight and I wanted to

185

watch? Our only TV is in the living room. Then I started thinking, Wait a minute . . . suppose my science teacher told us to watch a show on the Discovery Channel and we were going to discuss it in class tomorrow? She did that once. But this time I wouldn't be able to answer her questions. My teacher would say, *You should have told me you don't have a TV, Peter.* Then Sheila Tubman's hand would shoot up. *I happen to know the Hatchers have a TV, Ms DeFeo,* she'd blab. *It's in their living room.* Then I'd have to explain that I couldn't watch because our living room has been turned into a sleepaway camp. *What camp is that?* Mrs DeFeo would ask. And I'd have to think fast to come up with some name. *Camp Howie-Wowie,* I'd tell her. Then everyone would laugh.

The longer I thought about it, the more worked up I got. My heart started beating faster, my mouth felt dried out, and the palms of my

hands were getting clammy. Still, I couldn't tear myself away from the sleeping Howies. It was like one of those bad dreams where you want to run but you can't. It was like my feet were glued to the floor. I could feel the anger boiling up inside me. Any second I would burst and it would come pouring out like lava from a volcano. *Just go to bed,* I kept telling myself. But my feet refused to listen to my brain.

Finally, I forced myself to break away. I tore down the hall to the bathroom, shut the door behind me and leaned against it. But when I saw the five toothbrushes lined up in a row, the five towels hanging from the towel bar, and the five hairbrushes – not to mention the giant, economy sized bottle of vitamins – I just lost it. I mean, *totally*! I grabbed the towels and threw them to the floor, one after the other. Then I trampled them, like I was trying to kill some gigantic cockroach. *Aaaggghhhh!* This strangled

sound came from deep inside me as I swept their hairbrushes off the counter. I kicked at them as if they were poisonous snakes. *Aaaggghhhh!* I'd turned into a raving lunatic. No, even worse – I'd turned into my brother at the shoe store! Then I caught a glimpse of myself in the mirror. My face was red, my eyes wild. I looked like some demented guy in a scary movie. In the back of my mind I heard Cousin Howie asking, *What do we do when we get carried away?*

And the Natural Beauties answering, *We stop and count to ten.*

And if that doesn't work?

We count to ten again.

So I started to count. When I got to ten I took a deep breath, then started all over again. In the mirror I saw my facial expression return to normal. I couldn't believe I'd used Cousin Howie's method to control my anger. Or that it actually worked. But it did. I shook out the

five towels and hung them up again. Probably no one would notice since they were dark grey. *There are other ways to handle this situation,* I told myself, as I lined up their hairbrushes.

I marched down the hall to Mom and Dad's room and pushed open the door without knocking. 'How do we know these people are who they say they are?' I said.

Mom was stretched out on her bed, her hands over her eyes. 'What?'

'The Howies. They could be anybody. A week ago we didn't even know they existed and now they're sleeping on our living-room floor.'

'But they have the Hatcher jaw, don't they?' Mom said.

'I don't see any Hatcher jaw,' I said. 'Do you?'

'Well, I thought I did.' Mom looked worried for a second. Then she shook her head and waved her hand. 'Oh, this is silly. Of course they're Dad's cousins.'

189

'Hey, it's OK with me if you want five strangers sleeping on our living-room floor.'

'They're not strangers, honey,' Mom said. 'They're family. No one but Cousin Howie ever called Dad Tubby.' She put an arm around my shoulder. 'You should get to sleep.'

'I'd just like to know just one thing, Mom.'

'What's that?'

'Why you and Dad had to invite them to stay here? We don't have room for two extra people, let alone five.'

'They more or less invited themselves.' We were quiet for a minute, then Mom said, 'This is really important to Dad, so let's make the best of it, OK?'

'Important how?'

Mom said, 'When Dad was a boy his mother got very sick.'

'She did?'

Mom nodded. 'Cousin Howie's parents were

190

wonderful. Dad spent the whole summer with them. And for a while he and Cousin Howie were as close as . . . well, you and Jimmy.'

'How come I never heard this story before?'

'I guess Dad doesn't like to talk about that time in his life. It was hard on him.'

'Did his mother get better?'

'She did . . . for a while.'

'I wish Dad would tell me these things.'

'He doesn't like to upset you.'

'Yeah, but how am I supposed to understand anything if he won't talk about it?'

'Maybe someday he will,' Mom said.

'By then it'll be too late.'

'I hope not.' She reached out and ruffled my hair.

'I understand that having five *almost* strangers sleeping on the living-room floor doesn't give you, or any of us, much privacy. But it's just for a night. Two nights at the most.

We'll get through it.' Then she leaned over and kissed me. Sometimes I don't let her but this time I did.

I kept hearing Mom's voice saying, *It's just for a night. Two nights at the most.* When I woke up the next morning, the Howies were already in the kitchen, making themselves right at home – Eudora at the stove, scrambling eggs, Howie tending the toaster. Mini was seated on the counter next to the sink, breaking eggshells and sticking them to his nose and forehead. *This kid is as weird as Fudge,* I thought. The Natural Beauties were at the table, gobbling Dad's cereal. Fudge sat at his usual place, counting out his Cheerios.

Mom stood by, dressed in her whites, ready to go to work. She didn't look happy. I happen to know Mom doesn't like other people taking over her kitchen. She's OK with Grandma

192

cooking here, but that's her limit. Our kitchen isn't exactly roomy. We have a small table shoved up against the wall. You can reach the stove right from the table, which is sometimes convenient. But we eat most of our meals in the dining alcove.

I poured myself a glass of orange juice and took the last chair at the table.

'Good morning, Peter,' Eudora said. 'We've been talking about you.'

Me? What were they saying about me?

'We were just saying that maybe you could take Flora and Fauna to school with you today.'

What? I can't have heard right. I must have water in my ears from my shower.

'They'd like to see a New York City school,' Eudora continued.

This required quick thinking. 'My school doesn't allow visitors,' I said, hoping Mom would help me out of this one.

'That's right,' Mom told Eudora. 'They won't allow anyone in who hasn't previously registered. Schools have very strict policies in New York.'

'And tight security.' I threw that in just to make sure they got it. 'Besides,' I said to the Natural Beauties, who were filling their bowls with a second helping of Dad's cereal, 'I thought you're home schooled.'

'We are,' Flora began. 'But that doesn't mean—'

'We don't *visit* schools,' Fauna said. 'Besides, we've been studying—'

'Foreign cultures,' Flora said.

'This is New York,' I told them. 'It's not a foreign culture.'

'It is to us.' Fauna hiccuped. 'Sorry, it's the orange juice.'

'She's used to freshly squeezed,' Flora said.

Mom rolled her eyes and poured herself

a second cup of coffee.

I was trying to figure out if there's a pattern to the way the Natural Beauties speak. Does Flora start every time or only sometimes? Is Fauna the one who always finishes? So far I haven't been able to come up with anything clear. And trying to figure out who was saying what was making me tired even though my day had hardly begun.

Cousin Howie set plates of eggs and toast in front of each of the Natural Beauties. That's when he noticed Dad's cereal box and Flora's and Fauna's empty bowls. 'What have you girls been eating?' he asked, grabbing the box from the table. It was one of those cereals that promises to keep adults young and fit and regular. Cousin Howie began to read aloud from the list of ingredients on the side of the box. 'Artificial sweeteners? Artificial flavours?' He looked at the girls. 'Repeat after me, *I know*

better than to poison my body with unnatural ingredients.'

They repeated it.

'One more time,' Cousin Howie said.

'We know better than to poison our bodies with unnatural ingredients.'

'That's better,' he told them. 'Now eat your eggs.'

'But Daddy,' Flora began, 'we're not—'

'Hungry any more,' Fauna said.

'Not hungry?' Cousin Howie asked. *'Not hungry!'*

'That's what they said,' Fudge told Cousin Howie. 'Didn't you hear them?'

Cousin Howie's face turned red, then purple.

'Fudgie, let's remember our manners,' Mom said.

'I *am* remembering my manners. If Cousin Howie can't hear I'll help him, just like I help Mrs Osterman.'

'I can hear just fine,' Howie shouted.

Eudora said, 'Let it go, Howie. The girls will have a healthy breakfast tomorrow. Why don't *you* eat their eggs and toast instead.'

'You can sit here.' I jumped up to give him my place at the table.

'Thank you,' Cousin Howie said.

Turtle, who'd been under the table, looked up at Cousin Howie and whimpered, letting him know he'd be happy to share the eggs.

That's when Dad came into the kitchen carrying Tootsie. He sat her in her high chair. 'Os,' she said, pointing to Fudge's cereal box.

Dad sprinkled Cheerios on her tray.

Flora said, 'Oooooh, she's—'

'Soooo cute!' Fauna hiccuped loudly, making Tootsie laugh.

'Her name is Tamara Roxanne,' Fudge announced, 'and I'm not telling what we call her.'

'I'll bet I can guess,' Fauna said. 'Tammy?'

'Wrong,' Fudge sang.

'Roxy?' Flora guessed.

'Wrong again!'

'Mara?' Fauna tried.

'Nope!' Fudge laughed.

I was thinking they were all better names than *Tootsie*, but I didn't say so.

'Here's a hint,' Fudge said. 'It's the name of a candy.'

'We don't eat candy,' Flora said.

'Not even on Hallowe'en?' Fudge asked.

'Not even then,' Fauna said. 'That's why our teeth are—'

'Perfect.' Flora opened her mouth really wide so we could admire her teeth. 'We've never had a cavity.'

'But you eat ice cream,' Fudge said. 'I saw you.'

'And hot fudge,' I added, thinking we'd caught them.

198

'Daddy says ice cream is one of life's necessities,' Flora said.

'And hot fudge is a family tradition,' Fauna said.

'Daddy's very big on family traditions,' Flora said.

'Big!' Tootsie said, spreading her arms.

'So what do you call this precious girl?' Fauna asked.

'We call her . . . Tootsie!' Fudge announced.

'Too-zee,' Tootsie said.

'What an adorable—' Fauna began.

'Name,' Flora said. 'If we have a baby sister—'

'Maybe we can call her Tootsie,' Fauna said.

'Suppose you have a baby brother,' Fudge asked.

'Another brother?' Flora said.

We all looked over at Mini, just as he grabbed the sponge from the kitchen sink and stuffed it in his mouth.

'Farley,' Mom said, pulling it out, 'that's soapy.'

Mini looked right at Mom and growled.

The second I finished breakfast I was out of there. For once, I couldn't wait to get to school, where I wouldn't have to think about the Howies for the rest of the day. With any luck, they'd be gone by the time I got home.

Instead, halfway through homeroom period, as Mr Shane was making morning announcements, the door to our classroom opened, and the principal, Ms Rybeck, came in with two girls wearing dorky purple dresses.

This can't be happening, I told myself. *It's a bad dream. Any minute I'll wake up and start my day again. I know the Natural Beauties can't be at my school, standing in front of my homeroom class. I know it because we have tight security. Strangers aren't allowed.* I squeezed my eyes shut. *OK,*

200

I told myself, *when I open my eyes they'll be gone. The only person standing in front of the class will be Mr Shane. I'll count to three. I'll count really slowly. One . . . two . . . three.*

I opened my eyes but Ms Rybeck was still there, and she was introducing the Natural Beauties. 'Please welcome our distinguished visitors from Hawaii . . .'

Distinguished? I thought. *Now I know this must be a dream.*

'They are known throughout the Hawaiian Islands as the *Heavenly Hatchers*,' Ms Rybeck continued, 'and they have agreed to perform at a special school assembly later this afternoon.'

No . . . no . . . no! I could feel Jimmy and Sheila staring. *So, their last name is Hatcher. So what? There must be plenty of other Hatchers. I'll act as if this is just a coincidence. Please, Ms Rybeck, don't say they're related to me. Please . . . please . . . please . . .*

But did Ms Rybeck get my silent message? No, she did not. 'After an unexpected family reunion in Washington, D.C.,' she said, 'your classmate, Peter Hatcher, met his long-lost cousins, Flora and Fauna Hatcher, for the very first time.'

Why would the principal do this to me? What'd I ever do to her? If they start to sing 'The Best Things in Life are Free', I'll puke. I'll barf my guts out. Or maybe I'll get really lucky and just drop dead on the spot.

'Peter Hatcher?' Ms Rybeck said.

Since she doesn't know me personally, Ms Rybeck waited for me to raise my hand. But I didn't.

'Peter Hatcher?' Ms Rybeck said again.

Jimmy turned in his seat and gave me a quizzical look.

Finally Ms Rybeck asked, 'Is Peter Hatcher here this morning?'

Sheila's hand shot up. 'He's right over there, Ms Rybeck.' She pointed at me. Now all the kids turned and stared.

'Oh, good,' Ms Rybeck said.

I sank lower and lower in my seat, hoping if I slid down far enough I'd become invisible. Instead, I fell over and hit the floor.

Everyone laughed, including the Natural Beauties.

'I know it's exciting to have famous relatives, Peter,' Ms Rybeck said, 'but please try to control yourself. You'll be glad to hear that your cousins may accompany you to all your classes during their visit.'

On the way to first-period class, Jimmy Fargo called me Moonbeam. 'Hey, if you're related to the *Heavenly Hatchers* . . .'

'Cut that out!' I told him.

'Gotcha!' Jimmy said, laughing.

*

Just before assembly I excused myself to go to the nurse's room.

'What seems to be the problem?' she asked. She was a big woman, tall and heavy.

'Flu,' I said.

'What kind of flu?' she asked.

'Uh . . . temperature and headache.'

She popped a thermometer in my mouth and took my pulse. Then she took the thermometer out and read it. 'Normal,' she said. I could tell she wasn't impressed by my symptoms.

'And I feel really tired.' I yawned to show her *how* tired. 'So can I just stay here until assembly's over?'

'On another day I might go along with that,' the nurse said, 'but I really don't want to miss the *Heavenly Hatchers*. Come to think of it, didn't you sign in as Peter *Hatcher*?'

'Yes, but we're not related.'

'Really.'

'I mean, some people think we are but it's not true. It's a coincidence that we have the same last names.'

'Is that right? I could swear Ms Rybeck told me . . .'

'Oh, that's the other Peter Hatcher, the one in seventh grade.'

'And what grade are you in?'

'Uh . . . I'm in seventh, too.'

'Uh-huh.'

'OK, so we're some kind of distant relations, like eighteenth cousins seventeen times removed, something like that.'

'Interesting.'

'Please,' I begged. 'Please don't make me go. I don't think I can live through it. You don't want to be responsible for my sudden death, do you?'

'That bad, huh?'

'Could be,' I said.

'OK,' she said. 'But I don't want you moving off this bed. You understand?'

'Don't worry. I won't move.'

'I'll be back in ten minutes. I just want to hear their opening number.' She closed the door behind her and I let out a sigh of relief. I knew what was coming. I knew the Natural Beauties would be laughed off stage before they finished their first song. No middle schooler in New York City would be able to take the *Heavenlys* with a straight face. Kids in the first few rows would throw stuff at them. Leftover lunch – orange peels or cold and soggy French fries. This would go down in the history of our school as the day those weird sisters gave their final performance.

13
Do Not Pass Go

OK, so I was wrong. They weren't laughed off stage and nobody threw food at them.

The *Heavenly Hatchers* were a big hit. So what? That doesn't change my mind about them.

By the end of the day Sheila and the Natural Beauties were getting along like they'd known each other all their lives. Sheila could even tell them apart. 'It's easy,' she claimed on the way home from school. 'That is, if you're a person who notices details, which obviously you aren't, Peter.' Sheila invited them to stay overnight at her apartment. 'Since Libby's gone away to school I have a big room all to myself.'

Yes! I thought. *Go directly to Sheila's. Do not pass Go. Do not go back to my apartment. Ever.*

The Natural Beauties begged and pleaded but Cousin Howie wouldn't go for it. 'You know how we feel about sleepovers. You don't want to expose yourselves to bad influences, do you?'

I looked at the row of sleeping bags on our living-room floor and said, 'Isn't *this* a sleepover?'

'No, Peter, my boy,' Cousin Howie said, 'this is a family reunion.'

But Eudora said, 'You know, Howie, maybe it's not a bad idea to give our girls just an itsy-bitsy taste of freedom.'

'Spidah?' Tootsie asked, thinking Eudora was going to sing 'The Itsy-Bitsy Spider' with her.

Cousin Howie looked at Eudora as if she'd suggested something totally shocking. 'What are you saying, sweetheart?'

'I'm saying the sleepover would take place right in this building, just two floors away.'

'But what do we know about this Tubman family?' Howie asked.

I was thinking I could tell him plenty about the Tubmans, but before I had the chance Mom said, 'We've known the Tubmans for years.'

'We spent our summer vacation with them,' Dad added. 'Shared a house in Maine for three weeks.'

'My mother is *married* to Buzz Tubman's father,' Mom said. 'You can't get much closer than that.'

The Natural Beauties held their breath. I saw their fingers crossed behind their backs.

'What about their morals?' Howie asked. 'What about their values?'

Mom said, 'Morals?'

Dad said, 'Values?'

While Mom and Dad looked at each other I jumped in. 'Uh . . . excuse me . . . but I happen to know that Sheila thinks a lot about stuff like that.' I didn't add that she thinks my brother has *no* values.

'Aaaaand,' Fudge stretched out the word until he was sure he had everyone's attention. I knew he wouldn't be able to keep his mouth shut much longer. 'I might even marry Sheila,' he told the Howies. 'Last summer we played husband and wife.'

'Played husband and wife!' Howie said.

'It was an innocent game,' Mom said, trying to reassure Cousin Howie.

'We didn't even sleep in the same bed,' Fudge said.

'Sleep in the same bed!' Eudora cried.

'Neither did Grandma and Buzzy Senior,' Fudge added. 'Not until they got married. Now they play kissy-face all the time.'

'Kissy-face!' The Natural Beauties shrieked with laughter.

Mini licked Tootsie's arm. She petted his head the way she pets Turtle.

Finally, Howie and Eudora agreed to go

down to meet Sheila's family. They returned half an hour later with Sheila, and announced to Mom and Dad they'd decided to let the Natural Beauties have a sleepover. Sheila and the Natural Beauties hugged, then jumped up and down to celebrate the good news. I felt like jumping up and down, too.

'I'm still not entirely comfortable with the idea,' Cousin Howie told the Natural Beauties as they rolled up their sleeping bags and threw a few things into their backpacks.

'They'll be fine, Howie,' Dad said.

'If you don't mind, Tubby, I'll handle this myself.'

Dad raised his eyebrows but didn't say anything else.

'OK,' Cousin Howie said. His bulky frame blocked the door, so the Natural Beauties couldn't escape. 'First, I need some assurances from you.'

The Natural Beauties eyed each other.

'Number one . . .' Cousin Howie said, 'no pop music.'

I almost laughed.

But the Natural Beauties nodded and repeated, 'No pop music.'

'Number two . . .' Howie said, 'none of those fashion magazines with advice to the lovelorn.'

The Natural Beauties nodded again.

'Number three . . . no TV.'

'What do you mean by *no* TV, Mr Hatcher?' Sheila asked Cousin Howie.

'I mean *no* TV,' Howie said.

'Except *Sesame Street*,' Eudora added, smiling sweetly. '*Sesame Street* is OK, don't you think, Howie?'

'Tootsie watches *Sesame Street*,' Fudge said.

'We've *all* watched *Sesame Street*,' Sheila said.

'I don't approve of TV, period,' Howie said. 'It turns thinkers into vegetables.'

'What kind of vegetables?' Fudge asked. 'I like carrots and corn.'

'Never mind,' Cousin Howie said.

'Richie Potter likes broccoli,' Fudge told him.

'I *said* never mind,' Howie told him again.

'What about books?' Sheila asked. 'Books are OK . . . right?'

'None of those series books,' Howie told her.

'What about friends?' Fudge asked.

'Our girls are lucky to have each other,' Eudora said.

'I have Pete,' Fudge said, 'but I still like to choose my own friends.' He pranced around the living room. 'Know who my best friend is in mixed group? It's Richie Potter. Know who my best friend is in this building? It's Melissa Beth Miller. She lives in Jimmy Fargo's old apartment. Her cat's name is Fuzzball.' He dropped to the floor and crawled around, miaowing. 'Fuzzball's going to be a wizard for Hallowe'en.' Now he

was back on his feet, spinning. 'Know what I'm going to be for Hallowe'en?' He spun until he was so dizzy he fell to the floor. 'I'm going to be a miser. I'm wearing my money tie from Fudgington.'

Cousin Howie's mouth opened but no words came out.

Mini cried when the Natural Beauties left, until Mom promised him a sleepover, too.

'Where's he going?' Fudge asked.

'To your room,' Mom said, as Mini dragged his sleeping bag down the hall.

Fudge took Mom's hand and led her into the kitchen. 'I don't want Mini in my room.'

'He's our guest, Fudge,' Mom said. 'He looks up to you.'

'So?'

'So, sleeping in your room will be a treat for him.'

'He might lick my arm in the middle of the night.'

'Cousin Eudora says licking is Mini's way of kissing. It means he really likes you.'

'I don't want him to lick me.'

'You can keep your arms inside your blanket.'

'Suppose I forget?'

'Once he's asleep you'll be safe.'

'Suppose he doesn't go to sleep?'

'I guarantee he'll go to sleep,' Mom said.

'I still don't like it,' Fudge told her. 'Why can't he have a sleepover with Pete, instead?'

'Oh no,' I said. 'I stay up way too late for him. Besides, Turtle might bark all night.'

Mom settled it. 'Mini's going to sleep on the floor in *your* room, Fudge.'

'OK,' Fudge said. 'Then *I'll* sleep on the floor in Pete's room.'

'No way,' I told him. Then I went to my room, locked the door, and lay down on my bed with

the Dave Barry book I borrowed from Grandma. She says he's always good for a laugh and a good laugh was exactly what I needed.

With the Natural Beauties out of the way, Mini started talking for himself. His voice was such a surprise I looked around to see if maybe Fudge was talking for him, the way he had for Uncle Feather. But no, it was Mini himself, standing on Fudge's step stool, peering into Uncle Feather's cage. 'Nice bird,' he said.

'His name is Uncle Feather,' Fudge told Mini.

'Nice bird,' Mini said again.

'Call him Uncle Feather,' Fudge said. 'That's his name.'

'You're Uncle Feather,' Mini said, pointing at Fudge.

'No, I'm Fudge!'

'No, *I'm* Fudge,' Mini said.

'No, you're not!' Fudge told him. 'You're

Farley but we call you Mini.'

'No, *he's* Farley,' Mini said, pointing to me.

'No, *he's* Pete!' Fudge said.

'Who's Pete?' Mini asked.

'I give up!' Fudge shouted in frustration.

'No, I give up,' Mini said, laughing.

'You're a Turkey Brain!' Fudge shouted at him.

'Gobble gobble,' Tootsie said, as she toddled past Fudge's room.

It rained all weekend. Not that the Howies minded, because by Saturday morning they were hooked on TV. I'm not sure how it happened. It could be that on Friday night when Dad checked the Weather Channel, Eudora was intrigued. 'Why, look at that, Howie! Isn't that fascinating? You can follow the weather all over the country. They even show the Hawaiian Islands.' For the next two hours she and Howie

watched the Weather Channel. Then Howie got hold of the remote control and that was it. Talk about turning into vegetables! It was amazing. For all I know they pulled an all-nighter. I got up once to pee and could still see the flickering lights coming from the living room. I think they were watching reruns of *I Love Lucy*. They were laughing their heads off as if they'd never seen anything like it. I realized then, they probably hadn't.

Mom had to go to work on Saturday morning and Dad had his usual list of errands. But because of the heavy rain he didn't want to take Fudge or Tootsie with him. I knew what was coming. 'Peter, I won't be gone more than an hour. I've put Tootsie in for a nap. So if you can just keep an eye on Fudge . . .'

'Don't worry, Tubby,' Eudora said, yawning. 'I'll keep an eye on the little ones.' Cousin Howie

was surfing from Saturday morning cartoons, to the Weather Channel, to CNN *Headline News*, to a rerun of an Oprah special.

I went to check on Fudge. He was on the floor of his room, building a Lego rocket. Mini was back on the step stool keeping watch over Uncle Feather. 'Nice bird,' I heard him say.

As soon as Dad left, Turtle started barking at the door. That's what he does when he has to go out. I should have walked him when I first got up, but walking Turtle in the rain isn't exactly fun. I figured the Howies have three kids and another on the way. They could manage without me for fifteen minutes.

I pulled on my rain jacket and grabbed an umbrella. The second we were in the elevator, Turtle knew it was raining outside. Don't ask me how he knows, but he always does. He can smell it, I guess. He hates rain. When we reached the lobby I had to pull him towards the

door. When we got to the door, he whimpered. When I tugged on his leash, he lay down and rolled on to his back, trying to get me to feel sorry for him. He'll do anything not to set foot on wet pavement.

Henry watched, shaking his head. 'How's the bird?' he asked.

'The same.'

'Still not talking?'

'Not a word.'

I crouched down beside Turtle and talked to him very softly. 'Look, you have to do your thing, like it or not. It's not good for you to hold it in for so long.' He turned his head, pretending not to hear me.

Olivia Osterman offered a doggie treat. 'Thanks,' I said.

'He could be rebelling against his name,' she said. 'If he had a proper name like George or Rufus . . .'

'It's the rain,' I told her. Turtle sat up and ate his treat. I suppose I should have saved it for *after* he did his thing, as a reward. I held the umbrella over his head as I urged him outside. He cowered next to the building. 'OK. Fine. You want to do it here, go ahead, but we're not going back inside until it's done.'

For the longest time, he just stood there. Finally, when he realized I wasn't going to change my mind, he did it, without taking two steps away from the building. I scooped it into a baggie and threw the baggie in the trash basket. As soon as he was back inside, he shook himself off, spraying water everywhere, especially on me. All the way up in the elevator, he looked at me like I was beyond stupid for making him go out in the rain.

The minute I opened the door to our apartment, I was hit in the face by a flying Nerf Ball.

221

Everybody was racing around, screaming – Eudora in her nightgown, Cousin Howie in his pyjamas, Fudge, Mini, even Tootsie. 'What's going on?' I yelled. They were carrying on like it was the end of the world. Turtle took one look and ran, probably to hide under my bed.

I caught Fudge as he raced by. 'Pete!' he cried, 'Mini let Uncle Feather out of his cage, and Uncle Feather's going crazy.'

'He's not supposed to have free time unless Mom or Dad are home.'

'I know that.'

'So where is he?' I asked, just as Uncle Feather zoomed through the living room, dropping poop like miniature bombs. *Pow!* A direct hit on Cousin Howie's head. *Pow!* There goes the sofa. *Pow, pow, pow!* He hit the bookcase, the lamp and the coffee table.

My first thought was, *Mom's not going to be happy about this.* But then I thought, *Never mind*

the furniture, we have to protect Uncle Feather. I started shouting orders. 'Fudge, shut all the doors except to your room. Eudora, pull down the shades . . . fast! Cousin Howie, we need to get the mirrors covered.'

I ran for the closet where Mom keeps the old sheets, but tripped over Mini on the way. He was chasing Uncle Feather, arms outstretched, little hands in the air as if he could catch a bird bare-handed. 'Nice bird . . . nice bird . . .'

Tootsie followed Mini, calling, 'Peep . . . peep . . . birdie!'

I made it to the closet and tossed Fudge a sheet. 'Take that to Cousin Howie.' Instead, Fudge threw the sheet over his head and kept running, like a Hallowe'en ghost.

You could hear the thud when Uncle Feather crashed. He crashed into the kitchen window and fell, lifeless, to the floor. 'My bird!' Fudge cried.

Suddenly, it was absolutely silent in the apartment.

'Don't touch him,' Cousin Howie said. 'I've been trained to handle situations like this. Everybody stay calm. Fudge, get a blanket. We need to keep him warm.'

Fudge came back, dragging the queen-size blanket off Mom and Dad's bed.

'Something smaller,' Cousin Howie told him.

'A towel,' I said. 'Get a clean towel . . . the small kind.'

'And a box, please,' Cousin Howie said.

I ran into my room, dumped my baseball cards on my bed, then tore back to the kitchen with the box. 'We don't want to cause any harm,' Cousin Howie said. 'He has to be lifted very carefully.' Uncle Feather looked so small lying in the box. So still.

'Peter,' Cousin Howie said, 'do you know the vet's number?'

Mom keeps the emergency number for the twenty-four-hours-a-day animal hospital on the refrigerator. I picked up the phone and dialled. I don't think I did a very good job of explaining the situation. I managed to get out key words – *Myna bird. Crashed. Window.* I asked if there was a pet ambulance. The voice at the other end said we should bring him in ourselves.

'We'll take the van,' Cousin Howie said, throwing a rain poncho over his pyjamas. 'Eudora, stay here with the children. Peter, you come with me. I'll need a navigator who knows this city.'

'Don't forget the van keys,' Eudora said, tossing them to Cousin Howie.

'What about me?' Fudge asked. 'He's my bird.'

'Get your raincoat,' I told him. 'And hurry.'

The heavy rain made it hard to see, but the van was equipped with flashing red lights so at

225

least people could see us. I called out directions as Cousin Howie drove. 'Across Sixty-fifth Street through the park . . . to the East side . . . stay on Sixty-fifth until we hit York Avenue. It's on Sixty-second between York and FDR Drive.'

Fudge stroked Uncle Feather all the way to the animal hospital. 'He's going to be OK, right, Pete?'

'I hope so.'

'He has to be OK.'

'I know what you mean.'

'He can't die, right?'

'I just don't know, Fudge.'

'You have to know. You're the big brother.'

I choked up when he said that and moved closer to him. 'Please don't die, Uncle Feather,' he whispered. But Uncle Feather just lay there.

Cousin Howie dropped us off in front of the animal hospital. I carried Uncle Feather's box inside my rain jacket. Fudge clung to my

sleeve. The rain was still pouring down. So were Fudge's tears.

'Let's have a look,' the vet said, once we were inside the examining room. He unwrapped the towel. Uncle Feather looked up at him. 'Well, look at that,' the vet said, as if he was surprised to find a myna bird.

'His name is Uncle Feather,' Fudge said.

'Hello, Uncle Feather,' the vet said.

'Bonjour, stupid.'

At first I thought it was Fudge, imitating Uncle Feather's voice again. But when I heard it the second time, I was looking right at Fudge, and his lips never moved. The third time there was no doubt. 'Bonjour, stupid . . . stupid . . . stupid.'

The vet laughed and said, 'Bonjour to you, too!'

14
Dog Feet

Uncle Feather has a broken wing. He'll be in a splint for six weeks. If he'd crashed into the window headfirst, he might be dead now. Instead, he crashed sideways. The vet says he's a lucky bird. He should make a full recovery. In the meantime he's yakking away, making up for the weeks he didn't talk at all. Maybe flying into the window gave him something to talk about. Who knows what goes on in Uncle Feather's head.

I reached Dad on his mobile and he met us at the animal hospital. When he got there, Howie said, 'Well, Tubby, your boys handled this very well. Peter showed he can think fast in an emergency situation, and Fudge was calm and helpful.'

Dad hugged Fudge and me. 'I'm very proud of my boys, Howie.'

'You must be doing something right,' Howie said. 'Although I can't imagine what it is.'

When we got back home, the apartment was neat and clean, not a sign of bird poop anywhere. Eudora was dressed and making sandwiches for lunch, Tootsie was napping, and Mini was parked in front of the TV.

'And I don't want to hear one word about it, Howie!' Eudora said. 'He's watching the Discovery Channel.'

'Discovery Channel?' Howie said. 'Well, at least that sounds educational.'

'Yes, it is,' Eudora said. 'I'm sure our little Farley will learn a lot. And in case you were wondering, I've given Flora and Fauna permission to spend another night at the Tubmans'.'

'Well,' Cousin Howie said. 'I can see you're feeling perky today.'

'Yes, I am,' Eudora said. 'Very perky!'

We put Uncle Feather back in his cage and gave him some pear. He seemed confused at first, but not too confused to eat. 'You're a lucky bird,' Howie told him.

'Lucky, lucky,' Uncle Feather said.

Mini laughed. 'Bird talks.'

Cousin Howie held Mini in his arms so he could see inside the cage. 'You understand, don't you, that you can't let the bird out again?'

Mini didn't say anything.

'If you don't understand,' Howie said, 'you can't come into Fudge's room to watch his bird.'

Mini still didn't say anything, but he licked the side of Cousin Howie's face.

'Good,' Howie said. 'I'm glad you understand.'

That's it? I thought. *He thinks he can trust Mini*

230

just because Mini licked his face?

Fudge said, 'One time in Maine I let Uncle Feather out of his cage when it wasn't free time.'

'Then you understand the temptation, don't you, Fudge?' Cousin Howie said. 'And you don't blame our little Farley for what happened.'

'He shouldn't have done it,' Fudge said.

'You're right,' Cousin Howie said. 'Farley shouldn't have done it. But he's learned his lesson and he's never going to do it again. Isn't that right, Farley?'

'Lucky bird,' Mini said.

'Lucky bird . . . lucky lucky.'

'Uh . . . Cousin Howie,' I said, 'maybe we should have a rule that Mini can only watch Uncle Feather when someone's watching *him*.'

'Ordinarily I'd say that makes sense,' Cousin Howie said. 'But in this case it's not necessary.'

'Mini's not even four years old,' I said, in case Cousin Howie needed reminding.

'No matter,' Cousin Howie said. 'He understands.'

I could see there was no point in arguing with Cousin Howie.

After lunch Fudge pulled me aside and said, 'Let's play a game, Pete. How about Spit?'

'No, thanks.' It was a mistake for Sheila to teach him to play that card game. He thinks, instead of calling out the word *spit*, when he's out of cards, he's actually supposed to do it. He taught Richie Potter to play and they wound up having a spitting contest. It was disgusting.

'OK,' Fudge said, 'then how about Mono-Poly?'

'It's not Mono-Poly,' I told him. 'It's Monopoly. And you need more than two players to have a good game. Besides, you steal from the bank.'

'Come on, Pete, I won't steal.' He gave me his best-little-boy-in-the-world look.

232

'You promise?' I asked.

'I promise.'

I gave in, figuring if ever he deserved a reward for good behaviour this was it. Besides, I knew the game would be over in less than an hour. Playing Monopoly with Fudge is like playing basketball with your dog. He really doesn't get it. His only interest is in owning Boardwalk and Park Place.

'I'll buy that,' he said when he landed on Park Place today. He already owned Boardwalk but it was mortgaged. 'Plus, I'll buy two hotels.'

'You can't build houses or hotels until you pay off the mortgage,' I told him. ' Anyway, you don't have enough money to buy anything.'

'Oh, yes I do.' He pulled a wad of Fudge Bucks from his pocket.

'We only use Monopoly money when we're playing Monopoly.'

'OK, then I'll just make a quick stop at the cash machine.'

'There is no cash machine in Monopoly.'

'Well, there should be!' he argued.

'But there isn't,' I told him.

'Fine. I'll use my credit card.'

'What credit card?'

'The one Grandma gave me.'

'Grandma gave you a credit card?'

He pulled it out of his other pocket and waved it around. 'Too bad she didn't give one to you, Pete.'

'Let me see that.' I grabbed it out of his hand. 'This card is ten years out of date,' I said. 'Grandma should have thrown it away a long time ago.'

'I don't care!' Fudge said.

'Well, I do. And even if it was still good, you couldn't use it for Monopoly. This is a game, not real life.' I took my turn and landed on

234

Pennsylvania Railroad. I already owned it.

Then it was Fudge's turn. As he shook the dice, he started to sing, '*Oh, money, money, money, I love money, money, money.*' He threw the dice. Double fours. He moved eight spaces and landed on Community Chest. He picked up a card. 'Second prize in a beauty contest, Pete.' He held out his hand. 'Ten bucks, please.' Then he threw the dice again.

When Mom got home from work, Eudora had a big pot of chilli simmering on the stove and the table in the alcove set for dinner. Mom looked surprised and pleased. Eudora said, 'It's the least we could do. You've been so generous to us. And with the accident and all . . .'

'Accident?' Mom asked, and the expression on her face changed. 'What accident?'

'Oh, Anne,' Eudora said, 'I'm so sorry. I thought you knew.'

235

'Knew what?' Mom said, growing more worried. 'Is everyone all right?'

Fudge tore across the room and jumped into Mom's arms. 'It's Uncle Feather, Mom! He broke his wing. He has to wear a splint for six weeks. I helped Pete and Cousin Howie take him to the animal hospital. Did you know there's no ambulance for birds?'

'Wing?' Mom said. 'But how?'

Dad came into the room and put his arm around Mom. 'Uncle Feather's going to be all right,' he told her.

'But—'

'It's a long story, honey,' Fudge said, doing a perfect imitation of Dad.

Before Dad had the chance to fill her in on what happened, the doorbell rang. 'I wonder who that could be?' Mom asked.

She always says that instead of just opening the door and finding out for herself. While

236

she was wondering, I went to the door, looked through the peephole, and caught a glimpse of Jimmy and his father. 'Hey,' I said, opening the door. 'This is a surprise.'

'It's supposed to be,' Jimmy said. Then he helped Frank Fargo carry in a huge flat package wrapped in brown paper.

'For you,' Mr Fargo said, presenting it to Mom.

'For me?' Mom asked.

'Well, actually, for the whole family,' Mr Fargo said.

'What could it be?' Mom asked.

'See for yourself,' Mr Fargo told her.

'Come on, Mom,' I said, helping her tear off the brown wrapping paper.

'Oh, Frank!' Mom got all choked up when she saw what was inside. It was one of the paintings from his show – *Baby Feet Blueberry* – the original painting Tootsie walked across.

'We can't accept such a—'

Mr Fargo didn't wait for her to finish. 'Think of it this way, Anne,' he said. 'Without Tootsie, there wouldn't have been any show.'

'That's just what Dad says!' Fudge told Mr Fargo.

Dad turned red and laughed. 'It's fabulous, Frank, and more than generous.'

'It would look perfect over our living-room sofa,' Mom said. 'We've been saving for a piece of art, but with money being so tight these days . . .'

'What's *tight* money?' Fudge asked.

'Never mind,' Mom said.

'Come on, Mom. If it's about money I have to know.'

'Tight means there's not a lot to spend,' Mom explained, softly.

'Or it could mean somebody's really cheap,' I told him. 'Like a tightwad.'

238

'Thank you, Peter,' Mom said, and from her tone I knew I should stay out of this. 'But we're talking about a money situation here, not how a person *feels* about spending it.'

'I love it when we talk about money,' Fudge said. 'What's a wad?'

'This is hopeless,' Mom said.

'I can see that,' Mr Fargo answered. 'So let's skip the chit-chat and hang the painting.'

Dad helped Mr Fargo centre *Baby Feet Blueberry* over the sofa while Mom eyed it. 'A little higher . . . no, that's too high . . . about an inch lower . . . yes, that's it!'

Then we all stood back to admire the painting. Eudora said, 'Why, it looks as if it was meant to hang in that very spot.'

Cousin Howie said, 'Is it my eyes or are those swirls of colour moving?'

'They're supposed to look as if they're moving,' Mr Fargo said.

'Well, I'll be . . .' Howie said.

Then Fudge told Jimmy about Uncle Feather's accident and the three of us went to Fudge's room to check him out. Mini was standing on the step stool, watching over him. 'Nice bird,' Mini said. 'Lucky bird.'

'Nice bird . . .' Uncle Feather repeated. 'Lucky . . . lucky . . .'

'He's talking again?' Jimmy asked.

'Yeah,' I said.

'Just like that?'

'Yeah.'

'How come?'

'Nobody knows.'

'Nobody knows . . . nobody knows . . .'

'I know,' Mini said.

I looked at him. 'You know what?'

'Why the bird can talk.'

'Who told you?' I asked.

'The bird,' Mini said.

240

'The bird told you why he was talking again?'
I said.

Mini nodded.

'What did he say?' I asked.

'Can't tell,' Mini said.

'Why not?'

'Promised.'

'Promised who?'

'The bird!' Mini said. Then he laughed like crazy, sounding exactly the way Fudge did when he was that age. He was even starting to look like Fudge. How come I never noticed that before?

Fudge collected a stack of paintings from one of his shelves. He carried them into the living room and presented them to Mr Fargo. '*Dog Feet Red, Dog Feet Blue, Dog Feet Green* and *Dog Feet Purple.*'

Mr Fargo paid careful attention to each of Fudge's paintings. 'These are very good,' he

said. 'They show a lot of promise.'

I moved closer to check them out and what did I see? Paw prints. Every single painting was covered with paw prints! 'Wait a minute,' I said to Fudge. 'How did you get . . . ?'

Fudge laughed. 'It was so easy, Pete. Turtle liked walking across my paintings.'

'You used *my* dog for your paintings?'

'You want to buy one, Pete? They're for sale. Three zeros for each one.'

'You know how much three zeros adds up to?'

'Yeah, Pete,' Fudge said. 'More than two zeros!'

Jimmy invited me to go to supper and a movie with him and his father. I jumped at the chance to get out of the apartment. 'Maybe you can spend the night, too?' Jimmy asked.

'Yes!' I told him, before I even checked with

Mom and Dad. I knew they'd let me go. I knew they'd think by then I deserved a break.

The next morning, Giraffe Neck was at the Fargos' loft with Vinny. She made us French toast for breakfast. 'Wait till you taste it,' Jimmy said. 'It's the world's best. Right, Vinny?'

Vinny barked but this time he didn't retreat. He even let me pet him.

Sunday night, on the way home, Jimmy told me his dad and Giraffe Neck are getting married on Valentine's Day. 'And you have to be there,' he said, 'because I'm best man and I don't know anything about being best man.'

'You think I do?'

'Just promise you'll come.'

'OK, I promise.'

'Thanks.'

I was hoping that when I got home the Howies would be gone. And if not gone, then packing.

Instead, the Natural Beauties had returned and all five of the Honolulu Hatchers were lined up in their sleeping bags, out cold.

Two nights turned into four, four nights into seven. It was the longest week of my life, except for the time Fudge swallowed Dribble, my pet turtle. Finally, Dad said, 'Well, Howie, it's been wonderful getting to know your family but now—'

'I know, Tubby, and we feel as bad about leaving as you do. I know you wish we could stay longer.'

'But you're travelling around the country, and you still have a lot to see,' I said, hoping I was right.

'That was the plan,' Cousin Howie said. 'But plans sometimes change. And thanks to Henry Bevelheimer . . .'

Thanks to Henry Bevelheimer what?

244

'We're going to sublet the Chens' apartment while they're travelling in China. Which means we'll be your neighbours until the first of December.'

'But, but, but . . .' I began.

'Peter, my boy,' Cousin Howie said, 'no one understands better than me how hard it would have been to say goodbye. So even though we'll be separated by ten floors, we'll still be together for another six weeks.'

'Six weeks!' Fudge said. 'That's how long Uncle Feather's going to wear his splint.'

Six weeks! I thought. *No. . . no. . .* And I fell to the floor.

Fudge laughed. 'When Pete gets good news he always pretends to faint!'

15
Yelraf Rose

It was so great to have the apartment back to ourselves. It felt huge. It felt peaceful. Whoever thought life with my family could ever feel peaceful? No more wait to use the bathroom. No more hot dogs in rolls lined up on the living-room floor. With the Howies staying in the Chens' apartment, I'd hardly ever have to see them. Not only that, but the Natural Beauties aren't going to my school. They're taking dance classes and voice classes and drama classes all day, every day. *Yes!* I thought. *I have my life back.*

Dad proposed we celebrate our own small family by having dinner at Isola, our favourite neighbourhood restaurant. As soon as we walked in, I noticed Courtney, this girl from my

246

humanities class. She was with her family. 'Hi, Peter,' she said.

'Oh . . . uh . . . hi, Courtney.'

'Where are the *Heavenlys*?' she asked. 'I hope they're coming back to school soon. They are soooo cool.'

'They're not coming back to school.'

'That is soooo disappointing.'

I shrugged.

'Tell them Courtney from humanities said Hi.'

'I'll do that.'

As I walked away I heard Courtney telling her parents, 'That's Peter Hatcher. He's related to the *Heavenly Hatchers*. He is soooo lucky.'

As soon as I sat down at our table, Fudge asked, 'Is that your girlfriend, Pete?'

'No, that's *not* my girlfriend,' I told him. 'I don't *have* a girlfriend, and even if I did, I wouldn't tell you about her.'

'Don't worry, Pete. Someday you'll find one.'

'I'm not worried.'

'Because you're not *that* ugly.'

'Would somebody turn him off,' I said to my parents.

'That's enough, Fudge,' Mom said.

Tootsie banged on the table with a spoon. 'Eeee-nuf, Foo!' Then she threw the spoon. It just missed the waiter who was bringing us a basket of bread. Fudge helped himself to a piece, pushed out the middle, and stuffed it into his mouth. Mom handed his crust to Tootsie.

'Guess who came to mixed group today?' Fudge asked, his mouth so full he could hardly talk.

'Rumpelstiltskin?' I said.

Fudge laughed.

'Don't laugh with food in your mouth,' I told him.

'Why not?'

248

Mom and I answered at the same time. I said, 'Because it's disgusting.' Mom said, 'Because you could choke.'

'It was the Stranger Danger policeman,' Fudge said, after he'd chewed and swallowed. 'He showed us a video, then we all got secret code names. Only our family can know our secret code name. Want to hear mine?' He motioned for us to come close. 'I have to whisper so no one else can hear.' We leaned in. 'It's *Egduf Muriel*,' Fudge told us. 'Isn't that a good code name?'

'*Egduf?*' I said. 'What kind of name is that?'

'Shush . . .' Fudge said. Then he whispered again. 'It's Fudge spelled backwards.'

'Oh yeah . . . Fudge spelled backwards. Very clever.'

'What about the Muriel part?' Mom asked.

'That's how you get your code name,' Fudge explained. 'You spell your first name backwards,

and use your grandma's first name for your last name.'

'Suppose you have more than one grandma?' I asked.

'Peter,' Dad said, 'let's not make this more complicated than it already is.'

'Yeah, OK,' I said. 'But I don't get the point of this secret code name.'

'It's in case someone tries to steal me, Pete!'

'Steal you?' I asked. Who'd want to steal *him*?

'Yeah, Pete. Like some stranger comes up and says, *Your mom's in the hospital and I'm supposed to take you to see her.*'

Mom said, 'I never want you to go anywhere with a stranger, no matter what.'

'I know,' Fudge said. 'I don't talk to strangers, I don't get into cars with strangers, and I don't help strangers find their puppies. So there!'

'That's exactly right,' Mom told him. She

250

took a long drink of water.

'But just in case,' Fudge said, 'it's good to have a code name. So if a stranger *does* come up to me and says, *Please help me find my puppy,* I can say, *What's my code name?* And if he doesn't know it, I don't go with him.'

That got Mom really upset. 'Fudge, listen carefully,' she said. 'It doesn't matter what a stranger says. It doesn't matter if the stranger is a man or a woman or a teenager. If a stranger tries to talk to you, you shout, *I don't talk to strangers!* Then you run as fast as you can until you find someone you can trust – a policeman or a teacher or a . . . a . . .'

'Dog?' Fudge asked.

'Woof woof,' Tootsie said.

'Not a dog!' Mom told him. 'How could a dog help you?'

'That was a joke, Mom,' Fudge said.

Mom turned to Dad. 'I think I'd better have

251

a talk with William and find out what this is all about.'

'It's about Stranger Danger, Mom,' Fudge said. 'I already told you that.'

A few days before Hallowe'en the elevator in our building was converted to self-service. We've known for months it was going to happen. On the inside, the elevator still looks the same, with a mirrored wall and an upholstered bench. But now, instead of Henry running it, all you have to do is push a button to get to the floor you want. Henry says he's looking forward to his new job as supervisor of our building.

The best thing about the new elevator is the tiny video camera. It's supposed to be for security – or Stranger Danger, as Fudge says. This way, nobody can get into our elevator without Henry knowing about it. He can watch what's happening on a monitor in our lobby.

Anyone else who's interested can watch, too. At first everyone in the building stopped to have a look.

There's Mrs Tubman putting on her lipstick.

Isn't that Mr Perez tying his running shoes?

Ohhhh, the Reillys are kissing.

Hey, Gina Golden is adjusting her underwear!

It was like *Candid Camera*. Soon everyone wised up to the fact that they could be seen on the monitor. After that, the Reillys held hands but didn't kiss, and most people stopped checking themselves out in the mirror. Except Fudge. The minute he realized he could be seen on video, he started jumping up and down, waving his arms, and making stupid faces, usually with his tongue hanging out.

Henry called a meeting just for the kids in the building, especially since Hallowe'en is coming. The trick or treat sign-up sheet is already posted in the elevator. That's one great thing

about living in a high-rise in New York. You never have to leave your building to go trick or treating. Not that I'll be trick or treating any more. No. My trick or treat days are over. Makes me feel funny to think I'm too old for trick or treating. Reminds me of how I felt when I had my first double-digit birthday. *Ten*, I kept saying to myself. I'll be in double digits for the rest of my life – unless I live to be over one hundred. Yeah. That'd be cool – to get into triple-digit birthdays. Olivia Osterman might make it. If she does, and I ever get another dog, I'll name him George or Rufus, in her honour.

At the kids' meeting, Henry reminded us the videocam is for our security, not our entertainment, and he looked directly at Fudge. He demonstrated how to use the DOOR OPEN and the DOOR CLOSE buttons. He asked us to close our eyes and feel the numbers and symbols on the buttons. They were all in Braille

254

so people who are blind, like Mr Willard, can use the elevator on his own. Henry said anyone who pushes buttons just for fun will lose elevator privileges. He showed us how we could talk to him and he could talk to us in case there's an *incident*.

'What's an incident?' Fudge asked.

'Anything that's not supposed to happen in the elevator,' Henry said.

'What's not supposed to happen?'

'Let me put it this way, Fudge, the *only* thing that's supposed to happen is you push the button for the floor you want, the elevator takes you there, and you get out. Same as when I was running the elevator for you.'

Then he tested all the kids under twelve. If you passed Henry's test, you were allowed to use the elevator on your own. If you didn't, too bad. You'd have to take it again. Fudge passed on his first try.

'Does Mini have a code name?' Fudge asked Eudora. We were in the elevator on Saturday morning. Eudora was on her way to the park with Fudge and Mini. I was meeting Jimmy at the subway station. He was coming up to spend the day with me.

'What kind of code name?' Eudora asked Fudge.

'You know,' Fudge said, 'a *code* name. So nobody can steal him.'

'*Steal* him?' Eudora said.

'Yes.'

'Farley knows he's not supposed to talk to strangers,' Eudora said. Only Eudora and Howie still call Mini *Farley*.

'Yeah, but does he know if a stranger asks him to help find a puppy, he should run the other way, yell as loud as he can, and tell a *good* grown-up?'

256

Eudora grabbed Mini's hand. 'Right now I don't let him out of my sight when we're on the street.' She was quiet for a minute, then she asked Fudge if he had a code name.

Fudge nodded. 'A *secret* code name that only the family knows. You want to hear it?'

'Well, yes, I guess since I'm family I should know.'

'It's Egduf Muriel,' Fudge whispered.

'What an unusual name,' Eudora said. 'Isn't that an unusual name, Farley?'

'Egduf,' Mini said.

'Shush . . .' Fudge warned him. 'Never say it out loud.'

'Egduf,' Mini whispered.

'That's better,' Fudge said. 'In case you want to know what it means, it's Fudge spelled backwards.'

Eudora was quiet for a moment, then she said, 'Yelraf.'

'What?' Fudge asked.

'Yelraf,' Eudora repeated. 'That's Farley spelled backwards.'

'Now he needs a last name. Do you have a mother?' he asked Eudora.

'I did, but she died a few years ago. Her name was Rose.'

'You got that, Mini?' Fudge said. 'Your code name is Yelraf Rose, but it's a secret so don't tell anyone.'

'I think Mini's too young to get it,' I told Fudge.

'You're never too young for a code name, Pete. And never too old either. You better start working on yours if you're going to take the subway by yourself.'

'Thanks for the advice, Fudge.'

'Better safe than sorry! That's what Grandma always says.'

Not that I'd admit it to Fudge, but all his talk

about code names got me thinking maybe I should have one, too. *Hmmm, let's see.* I spelled my name backwards in my head. *Retep.* Then I threw in my middle name spelled backwards just to make it more interesting. *Nerraw.* Then I added Grandma's name. *Muriel.* That made me Retep Nerraw Muriel. Good name. But who should I tell? Not Fudge – he'd broadcast it to the world. Jimmy? I don't think so. He might laugh. I still couldn't figure out how having a code name would help if I met up with trouble on the subway or any place else.

As soon as the Howies were settled in the Chens' apartment, Eudora invited us down to dinner.

'Do I have to go?' I asked Mom.

'Yes.'

'Can't you tell them I have a stomach ache or something?'

'No.'

'Can I go home the second I'm done eating? Because I have a lot of homework.'

'You can go home as soon as the table is cleared,' Mom said. 'As long as you're polite about it.'

'I'll be very polite. You wouldn't believe how polite I can be when I want to be polite. I'll be so polite—'

'OK, Peter,' Mom said. 'I get your point.'

At the dinner table, the talk turned to Hallowe'en. Fudge said, 'Mini can trick or treat with me.'

'We're taking him,' Flora said. 'We've always been curious about—'

'Hallowe'en,' Fauna said.

'What's all this talk about Hallowe'en?' Howie asked. 'You know how I feel about candy.'

'We don't care about the—' Fauna began.

'Candy,' Flora interrupted. 'We're interested in the cultural—'

260

'Event,' Fauna said. 'We want to—'

'Observe,' Flora said, 'as part of our—'

'Studies,' Fauna said.

Mom told Cousin Howie how safe it is to trick or treat in our building. 'We know all the neighbours.'

Eudora said, 'It might be educational for them to experience Hallowe'en one time, Howie.'

Cousin Howie drummed his fingers on the table. His eyebrows crept together. After a while he said, 'All right, but just this one time. And no candy. Candy will rot your teeth.'

'You don't have to worry about candy, Daddy,' the Natural Beauties said together.

I was beginning to see how this worked. Cousin Howie said No to everything. The Natural Beauties begged and pleaded. Eudora was usually on their side. She had to present the case very carefully to Howie. But in the end, the Natural Beauties almost always got their way.

'What's Mini going to be for Hallowe'en?' Fudge asked.

'He's going to be a—' Flora began.

'Tiger,' Fauna said.

Mini growled.

'Or maybe a—' Flora began again.

'Lion,' Fauna said.

Mini growled, louder this time.

'I know,' Flora said. 'He wants to be a—'

'Manatee,' Fauna guessed, sure she got it right this time.

'No!' Mini shouted, surprising everyone. 'Egduf.'

'Egduf?' Flora said. 'What's an egduf?'

'It's me!' Fudge told them. 'Mini wants to be *me* for Hallowe'en.'

'You?' the Natural Beauties said at the same time.

'Yes,' Fudge told them. 'Yelraf Rose wants to be Egduf Muriel.'

262

'Does anybody know what's going on here?' Howie asked.

'I do,' Eudora said. 'And it makes perfect sense.'

On Hallowe'en night the Natural Beauties brought Mini up to our apartment. Fudge was already dressed as a miser in a white shirt, a pair of red braces and his money tie from the Bureau of Printing and Engraving. He carried his pouch of shredded money in one hand, and in the other, his trick-or-treat bag.

Mom had another white shirt ready for Mini, along with a second pair of red braces. Since there was only one money tie, Mom let Fudge decorate an old green tie of Dad's. He drew dollar signs with wings all over it. Mom plonked a man's hat on each of their heads. Then she snapped photos of the two of them – the miser and his double.

The doorbell rang. It was Melissa Beth Miller from downstairs. She was carrying her cat in a basket. Fuzzball was wearing a pointy black hat. 'He's my wizard,' she said. 'And I'm Hermione from—'

'Don't say it out loud!' Fudge shouted.

'Don't worry,' Melissa said. 'I never say *his* name out loud.'

'Whose name?' Flora asked.

'Never mind,' I told them. This was all getting to be too much for me.

'OK, Pete, let's go!' Fudge said.

'Go?' I asked.

'Yeah. You're taking me and Melissa.'

'Wait a minute. I thought you were going with Flora and Fauna.'

'No, they're taking Mini.'

'We couldn't possibly be responsible for more than one child,' Fauna said.

'Because we'll be busy taking notes for our

report on the cultural event,' Flora told me.

'Daddy says we each have to write three pages,' Fauna said.

'Single spaced,' Flora added, in case I still didn't get it.

'OK, OK,' I said. 'Let's just go and get this over with.'

We all took the elevator to the sixteenth floor and started working our way down. At every apartment the Natural Beauties sang a few lines from their collection of New York songs – 'East Side, West Side'; 'Forty-Second Street'; 'Give My Regards to Broadway'; 'Manhattan'. The neighbours loved it. They tried to shower the Natural Beauties with candy but they politely refused.

On the sixth floor we met up with Olivia Osterman, who was just coming out of her apartment. She was wearing a long red cape. 'I'm going to a party,' she said, holding a

265

feathered bird mask in front of her face.

'You look like Uncle Feather, except you're the wrong colour,' Fudge told her.

'I'm a nightingale, not a myna,' Mrs Osterman said as she pressed the button for the elevator.

The Goldens, who also live on six, opened their door. Mr and Mrs Golden and their daughter, Gina, were all wearing fright wigs. 'Happy Hallowe'en!' they sang together. They had vampire teeth in their mouths. Mini growled at them. Before the Natural Beauties could get out two notes, the Goldens' poodle started barking at Fuzzball. Fuzzball leaped out of the basket and ran for his life, straight into the Goldens' apartment. 'Fuzzball, come back here!' Melissa called, chasing him. Mrs Golden ran after Melissa, and Gina ran after Mrs Golden. Mr Golden just stood there in his fright wig and vampire teeth, holding the bowl of candy bars.

'How many?' Fudge asked.

'How many *what*?' Mr Golden said.

'Candies,' Fudge said. 'How many can I take?'

'How about one?' Mr Golden said.

'How about two?' Fudge asked.

'OK,' Mr Golden said. 'Two.'

'Mini doesn't have a bag,' Fudge told Mr Golden. 'So I'll also take two for him.'

Mr Golden said, 'Four candy bars is a lot of candy.'

'Not really,' Fudge argued, 'because you said I could take two. Besides, Peter and Flora and Fauna aren't taking any. So it's a real bargain.' He reached into the bowl again. 'But I better take two for Melissa in case she forgets.'

'What are you, an entrepreneur?' Mr Golden asked.

'No, I'm a miser.' He pointed to Mini. 'And he's my double.'

'Egduf,' Mini said.

Mr Golden just shook his head.

Melissa couldn't find Fuzzball anywhere in the apartment. Mrs Golden asked me and the Natural Beauties to help look for him. I don't know how long it took to find Fuzzball, but I know it was too long. Way too long. Because by the time we found him – on top of a stack of towels in the bathroom closet – Fudge and Mini were nowhere in sight.

'Did you see them leave?' I asked Mr Golden, who was offering the bowl of candy to another group of kids.

'Who?' Mr Golden asked.

'The misers,' I told him. When he looked blank I added, 'The little kids in the red braces.'

'Oh, they left a long time ago.'

'This is bad news,' Flora cried.

'We're going to be in so much trouble,' Fauna said.

268

'What'll we do?' they asked together.

'First we'll take Melissa home,' I said, taking charge.

'But I'm not done trick or treating,' Melissa said.

'Maybe you're not, but your cat is,' I told her.

'He's not my cat, he's my wizard.'

'Either way, it's time for him to go home.'

I pressed the button for the elevator. Then we waited. And waited. And waited. Finally, I said, 'Come on, we'll take the stairs.'

I led them down the back stairway. We met other groups of trick or treaters along the way. One of the fathers said, 'Whew, these stairs are tough going.'

Another one muttered something about the new elevator.

'Yeah, I know,' I told him. 'We waited on six but it never came.'

'Probably all those trick or treaters,' he said.

269

In the lobby a group of neighbours had gathered around the video monitor. 'Henry,' I said, 'you haven't by any chance seen . . .'

He pointed to the monitor.

I looked at the screen. But it was so dark you had to look really carefully to see anything. You could just make out somebody sitting on the bench waving a pencil flashlight. Wait a minute, was that a bird mask? The light moved and landed on Mini's face.

'What's going on?' I asked Henry.

'They're stuck between floors,' Henry said.

'Oh no!' the Natural Beauties cried.

The light moved again and caught the control panel. You could see a small hand, then part of a face. It was Fudge.

'Can't you do something?' I asked.

'Shush . . .' Henry said. 'He's trying to use the intercom.'

'This is Egduf Muriel, Yelraf Rose and Aivilo

Veruschka,' Fudge said in a small voice.

Aivilo? I thought. Then I realized Aivilo spelled backwards is Olivia. So it *was* Olivia Osterman.

'This elevator won't go anywhere,' Fudge said. 'It won't go up and it won't go down. And besides that, it's dark in here. And hot.'

A buzz went through the group around the monitor. 'Quiet, please!' Henry called. Then he pressed his talk button. 'Are you all right, Mrs O? Can you breathe?'

'She looks like a bird breather with her mask,' Fudge said.

'Can you get us out of here?' Mrs Osterman asked, very politely. 'Hallowe'en comes just once a year, you know. And who knows where I'll be a year from now?'

'Help is on the way,' Henry said.

'Will it be the fire department?' Mrs Osterman asked. 'I've always wanted to be rescued by one of those handsome young men.'

'They should be here any minute,' Henry said. 'Along with the elevator maintenance crew.'

'Don't worry,' Fudge said. 'We're not hungry. We still have forty-seven candy bars to go.'

'Yum,' Mini said and we could see him eating one.

The Natural Beauties asked Henry if they could talk to Mini. Henry pressed his talk button.

'Mini, it's Flora.'

'And Fauna. We love you. Don't be scared.'

'He's not scared,' Fudge said. 'Nobody's scared.'

'We're going to sing now,' Mrs Osterman announced. 'You can listen to our special song.' The three of them began to sing to the tune of 'Frère Jacques'.

Egduf Muriel, Egduf Muriel
Yelraf Rose, Yelraf Rose

272

Aivilo Veruschka, Aivilo Veruschka
Touch your nose,
Or your toes . . .

Word about the elevator spread through the building. Mom and Dad heard it from one of the trick or treaters who came to their door. They ran down all twelve flights of stairs. Howie and Eudora heard it at about the same time. Cousin Howie pushed through the crowd, which had grown. 'I'll take charge now, Henry. I'm a park ranger. I know what to do in case of emergencies.'

'Sorry, Cousin H,' Henry said, 'but in this case, I'm in charge. And I've turned the operation over to the fire department and the emergency elevator-maintenance team. They're on the scene now.'

'How long have they been trapped in the elevator?' Dad asked.

273

'Close to forty minutes,' Henry said.

'Oh . . .' Eudora moaned.

'Water,' Mom called. 'Somebody bring her a glass of water.' And she helped Eudora to a chair.

'I want to talk to my son,' Dad said.

'Sure thing, Mr H.' Henry put Dad on the intercom.

'Fudge, this is Dad. Talk to me, please.'

'Hi, Dad,' Fudge said. 'Aivilo taught us this game.'

'Aivilo?' Dad said.

'That's Olivia spelled backwards,' I whispered.

'See, first you think up an animal,' Fudge said, describing the game to Dad. 'And then you try to make the others guess which animal it is. I did panda and Mini guessed it.'

'Sounds like a good game,' Dad said. 'How is Mini?'

'He's resting now.' Fudge shone Mrs

274

Osterman's flashlight on Mini. He was stretched out across the bench, his head in Mrs Osterman's lap. She was fanning him with her bird mask. 'Fudge, let me talk to Mrs Osterman,' Dad said.

'Hello, dearie,' she said. 'Don't worry. We're all right. Just a bit anxious. We'd like to be out of here.'

'Dad,' Fudge said, 'guess how many candy bars Mini ate?'

'Candy?' Cousin Howie said.

'Seven so far,' Fudge said. 'But now he has a tummy ache. That's why he's resting.'

Cousin Howie grabbed the intercom. 'Farley, no more candy. Got that?'

But before Mini could answer, the lights in the elevator came on, and we could hear the whirr of a fan.

'Oh my!' Mrs Osterman said. 'That feels good.'

Then a guy in uniform dropped into the

elevator from a hatch in the ceiling. We heard a noise, and a minute later Fudge said, 'We're moving!'

'And just in time, dearie,' Mrs Osterman said. 'Just in time.'

When the elevator door opened, a handsome firefighter escorted Mrs Osterman out, with Fudge and Mini following right behind. 'Make room for Mrs O,' Henry called and the crowd parted.

'Well,' she said, 'I see I didn't miss the party after all. The party seems to be right here in the lobby!'

As soon as she said it, you knew it was going to happen. Within minutes the neighbours were carrying food and drinks to the lobby. The trick or treaters followed. Mr Reilly brought down his keyboard. The Natural Beauties ran upstairs and returned with their tap shoes.

Mr Willard proposed a toast. 'To our heroes Olivia, Fudge and Mini.'

'You mean Aivilo, Egduf and Yelraf?' Fudge asked.

'Yes,' Mr Willard said. 'That's exactly who I mean.'

Mr Reese said, 'Here's to their resourcefulness . . .'

Mrs Perez said, '. . . And to their sense of humour.'

'Three cheers for Egduf, Yelraf and Aivilo!'

While we were cheering, the lobby door opened, and the Tubmans came in from outside. They were dressed as the Three Bears. 'What's going on?' Sheila asked. 'Did I miss something?'

'Candy,' Mini said. 'Yum!'

16

You Never Know

After Hallowe'en the weather turned cold. The
Natural Beauties had never experienced winter.
Whenever I saw them they were shivering.
So was Mini. Since they'd be on their way to
Florida soon, Cousin Howie said it didn't make
sense to buy winter clothes. I kept thinking if
they were *that* cold, they'd leave New York and
head south before their six weeks were up. But
the Natural Beauties were determined to stay in
New York until the last possible moment.

Mom and Mrs Tubman put together a box
for them. Sweaters and jackets for the kids, and
winter maternity clothes for Eudora. She was
growing now. You could definitely tell she was
pregnant. Fudge loved putting his hands on her

belly. 'There's really a baby inside?'

'Yes,' Eudora said.

'Just like a panda.'

'Not quite like a panda,' Eudora said. 'Panda babies are no bigger than the palm of my hand when they're born. My baby will be at least six or seven pounds. You remember Tootsie when she was born, don't you?'

'I didn't like her,' Fudge said.

'But you like her now,' Eudora said.

'Not as much as I'd like a panda.'

'Pan-da,' Tootsie said.

'That's right,' Eudora said. 'You're getting to be quite a talker.'

And she wasn't the only one. 'I can talk, too,' Mini announced to the Natural Beauties.

'We know you can,' Flora said.

'But you don't have to,' Fauna said.

'Because you have us,' Flora said.

'No!' Mini shouted.

'What do you mean?' Fauna asked him.

'I think he means—' Flora began.

'Stop!' Mini said.

'Stop?' Fauna asked.

'I can talk myself!'

'Is he saying he doesn't want us to talk for him any more?' Flora asked.

'Is that what you're saying, Mini?' Fauna asked.

'Yes.'

'I guess he's growing up,' Flora said.

'I guess he's not our *baby* brother any more,' Fauna agreed, sounding sad.

'Cheer up,' Fudge told them. 'Soon you'll have another baby in the family. It might even be a panda baby.'

'A panda baby?' The Natural Beauties laughed.

'You never know,' Fudge told them. 'Mrs Little had a mouse. She named him Stuart.'

Fudge has his first loose tooth. Bottom front. He's planning on collecting big-time from the tooth fairy. He's been wiggling his loose tooth for weeks. He was still wiggling it at our farewell dinner with the Howies. Mom invited Olivia Osterman, too, so the three heroes could have a reunion. But Mini was more interested in Uncle Feather than a reunion. He took off for Fudge's room right away. I was glad to see Cousin Howie follow him.

Once the Natural Beauties found out Olivia Osterman had been a Broadway star, they wanted to hear everything about her life on stage. 'New York is a magical place,' she told them. 'It's a city where your dreams can come true. Where a girl can become a star overnight.'

That was enough for the Natural Beauties. 'Please . . . please . . . please . . .' they begged

281

Eudora. 'Can we *please* stay in New York? You and Daddy can go south, and we'll come down to visit.'

'That's out of the question,' Eudora told them. 'You belong with your family.'

The Natural Beauties looked at Mom.

Oh no! I thought.

'Please, Cousin Anne,' Fauna begged. 'We wouldn't be any—'

'Trouble,' Flora said.

'No, no, no!' Eudora said. 'That's not what I meant.'

But the Natural Beauties had their own ideas. 'We'd help out with—'

'Tootsie,' Fauna said.

'What about me?' Fudge asked. 'Don't you want to help out with me?'

'Sure,' Flora said. 'With you, too.'

'Girls . . .' Eudora told the Natural Beauties, 'that's enough!'

'Enough of what?' Howie asked, returning with Mini.

'Never mind,' Eudora said.

Mom thanked the Natural Beauties for their kind offer. 'Wasn't that a kind offer, Warren?'

Dad nodded but he looked worried until Mom said, 'Unfortunately, girls, this isn't the right time for us to take on any more responsibilities.'

'Well, of course it isn't,' Eudora said.

'Besides,' Dad said, 'winter is long and hard, and you're not used to it.'

'But we'd love to see snow,' the Natural Beauties said at the same time.

'What are we talking about here?' Cousin Howie asked.

'About college,' Dad said, thinking fast. 'Maybe when Flora and Fauna are older, they can come to New York to study.'

'And live in a dorm,' I added.

'Yes,' Mom said, 'they wouldn't want to miss out on dorm life.'

I bowed my head and silently gave thanks that Mom and Dad are smarter than I thought.

'Dorm life?' Cousin Howie said. 'I don't know about that. I've read they have co-ed dorms these days.'

'Well, we don't have to worry about that yet, do we?' Eudora said.

A minute later Mom announced that dinner was ready, and we took our seats at the table. 'Let's all join hands and give thanks,' Cousin Howie said.

I wasn't about to tell him I already had.

We went around the table, taking turns. Cousin Howie gave thanks for finding his long-lost family.

Mrs Osterman gave thanks for an interesting life.

The Natural Beauties gave thanks for New York.

Mini gave thanks for Egduf, then leaned over and licked Fudge's arm. Fudge inched away and pulled down his sleeves.

Then it was Fudge's turn. 'I give thanks for money,' he said.

Dad sighed. 'Can you think of anything else, Fudge?'

'Toys?' Fudge said.

'I'll bet there are other things you're thankful for,' Dad said.

'Oh, *those* things,' Fudge said, and he started listing all of them. 'I give thanks that Uncle Feather can talk again, and that his wing is better, and that I'm smart, and Mom and Dad love me best.' He looked right at me. 'Ha ha, Pete!'

'Ha ha,' I said.

But he still wasn't finished. 'Aaannndd, I give

thanks for monster spray and for my teacher, William, and Grandma and Buzzy and Richie Potter . . . and . . . and . . . and . . .'

He went on and on, but I tuned him out and thought about all the things I'm thankful for. Not that I'd say any of them out loud in front of the Howies, or anyone else. Not everything has to be announced to the world. Some things are private. I guess Fudge hasn't learned that yet because he was still going strong, giving thanks for his favourite books, his favourite foods, even his favourite smells.

Finally, Dad said, 'Thank you, Fudge. I think we can eat now.'

While we were eating, Cousin Howie waved his fork around and explained to Mrs Osterman that they'd be heading for the Florida Everglades in a few days.

'Everblades?' Fudge perked up. I've told him a million times it's *glades* not *blades*, but he still

286

doesn't get it. He has the idea that the Howies are going to a place where nobody walks, bikes or drives. They just blade. 'Is that near Disney World?' he asked. 'Because I really want to go to Disney World. I'm thinking of buying it.'

Cousin Howie laid down his fork and wiped his mouth with his napkin. 'Tubby, you've got to bring your family down to visit. You've got to let me show them the *real* Florida, the one nature created, not Mr Disney. We'll do a canoe trip through the Everglades. They'll see alligators and crocodiles.' Cousin Howie turned to Fudge. 'Did you know, little fella, it's the only place in the world where alligators and crocodiles live together?'

'And all kinds of birds,' Fauna added.

'We have birds in New York,' Fudge said. 'We have pigeons.'

'No offence, Fudge, but we're not talking about pigeons,' Cousin Howie said. 'We're

287

talking about flamingos and herons and spoonbills.' Cousin Howie turned to Dad. 'So what do you say, Tub, how does Christmas in the Everglades sound?'

'Not Christmas,' I said, quickly. 'We always have Christmas in New York.'

'Then February,' Cousin Howie suggested.

'Not February,' I said. 'I can't leave town in February. Jimmy Fargo's father is getting married on Valentine's Day, and I promised I'd be there.'

'Never say *can't*, Peter,' Cousin Howie told me. 'Where there's a will, there's a way. I'll bet you've heard that before.'

'I've heard it!' Fudge sang. 'From Grandma.'

'Good,' Cousin Howie said. 'Then it's settled. A family reunion in the Everglades sometime this winter. Some week when you want to get away from the ice and snow, the howling winds and the grey skies.'

288

'Well,' Mom said. 'That's a very kind invitation, and we certainly appreciate it.'

'It may not be *this* winter,' Dad said, 'but you can be sure it will be *some* winter.'

Yeah, I thought. *Like in fifty years.*

For dessert we had brownies with ice cream. Fudge bit into a brownie, then got this funny look on his face. He reached into his mouth and pulled something out. 'Look, everybody!' he said, holding it up. 'A chocolate-covered tooth!'

'Put it under your pillow tonight and the tooth fairy will come,' Mrs Osterman said. 'But wash it off first.'

When dinner was over and Dad was clearing the dessert plates, Fudge looked around and said, 'Where's my tooth? I put it right here on the table and now it's gone. Did you take it, Dad?'

'No,' Dad said.

'Did you take it, Pete?'

'No,' I said. 'Why would I take your tooth?'

'Then where is it?' Fudge asked.

I almost said, *With your missing shoe and your green marble*, but I didn't. We still haven't found his green marble. And for all we know, his missing shoe is still riding some subway train.

'Maybe your tooth fell on the floor,' Mom said.

Fudge got out of his seat and searched for it. But no luck. 'It was next to my milk glass. Mini saw it, didn't you, Mini?'

Mini nodded.

'Mini,' Flora said, 'do you know where Fudge's tooth is?'

Mini nodded again.

'Tell him where it is,' Fauna said.

'Gone,' Mini said.

'Gone where?' I asked.

Mini patted his stomach.

Cousin Howie laughed. 'He's making a

joke. Isn't that right, Farley?'

'No,' Mini said.

'I want my tooth,' Fudge told him. 'I want it now!'

Mini laughed and patted his stomach again.

'What are you trying to say, Mini?' Fauna asked.

'Egduf's tooth.'

'What about Egduf's tooth?' Flora said.

Mini climbed out of his chair and raced around the table, singing, '*Yummy, yummy, yummy . . . tummy, tummy, tummy . . .*'

Fudge let out a wail. 'Noooo!'

Eudora jumped up from the table. 'You didn't really swallow Fudge's tooth, did you, Farley?'

Mini kept on running around the table. 'It tasted like chocolate.'

'Mom! Dad!' Fudge yelled. 'Do something!'

This was beginning to sound familiar. *Way too familiar.*

Cousin Howie was out of his seat in a flash. He caught Mini and turned him upside down.

'Howie,' Eudora warned, 'he just finished dinner.'

But Cousin Howie whacked him on his back anyway. No tooth came out and, lucky for us, neither did anything else.

'Now the tooth fairy won't come!' Fudge cried. He might have torn Mini apart to get his tooth back, but the Howies were out of the apartment so fast you'd have thought the place was on fire. The second they were gone, Fudge cried, 'I hate Mini! First my bird and now my tooth. He's a disaster.'

'Now you know how I felt,' I said.

'What do you mean, Pete?'

'When you swallowed Dribble, my turtle.'

Fudge thought about that. 'Did you hate me, Pete?'

'Yeah, I did.'

'Was I a disaster?'

'Yeah, you were.'

From the other room we could hear Uncle Feather calling, 'Disaster . . . disaster.'

'But I'm not any more, right?' Fudge asked.

I didn't say anything.

'You're really glad I'm your little brother now. I'm the best little brother you could ever have, right?'

I still didn't say anything.

'If you say *yes*, I'll show you my secret.'

I snorted. I knew he'd show me his secret no matter what I said.

Later, when he went to bed, Fudge tucked a note to the tooth fairy under his pillow. Mom and Dad helped him write it, explaining the situation.

'Psst, Pete,' he called as I was passing his room.

'What?'

He motioned for me to come in and sit on his bed. 'Look what I found.' He pulled a small box out from under his pillow.

'What's this?' I asked.

'Open it and you'll see my secret.'

I opened the box. It was full of tiny teeth. 'Where'd you get this?'

'I found it in Mom's room.'

'These must be *my* teeth,' I said.

'But the tooth fairy won't know, will she?'

'Yeah, she will,' I told him. 'And she'll never trust you again.'

I grabbed the box and took it to my room. I lay down on my bed, trying to remember how it felt to be Fudge's age. I touched the tiny teeth. Then I slipped the box under my pillow – because, hey, you never know.

Acknowledgements

Many thanks to Dr Bob Hoage – Chief, Office of Public Affairs at the National Zoo in Washington, D.C. – for an up close and personal tour that Elliot and I will always remember. Thanks, too, for driving safely and carefully, *nothing* like Cousin Howie! And thank you to Lisa Stevens, Assistant Curator for Pandas and Primates at the National Zoo, not only for introducing us to Mei Xiang and Tian Tian, but for giving me the idea for The Panda Poop Club.

About the Author

Judy Blume spent her childhood in Elizabeth, New Jersey, making up stories inside her head. She has spent her adult years in many places, doing the same thing, only now she writes her stories down on paper. More than 82 million copies of her books have been sold, in thirty-two languages. Her twenty-eight books have won many awards, including the National Book Foundation's Medal for Distinguished Contribution to American Literature.

Judy lives in Key West, Florida, and New York City with her husband. She loves her readers and is happy to hear from them. You can visit her at JudyBlume.com, follow @JudyBlume on Twitter or join her at Judy Blume on Facebook.